BRIDGING BETWEEN

Spirit's Energy Transformation
Reset for Mother Earth

L T BAILEY

BALBOA.PRESS

A DIVISION OF HAY HOUSE

Balboa Press books may be ordered through booksellers or by contacting:

Balboa Press
A Division of Hay House
1663 Liberty Drive
Bloomington, IN 47403
www.balboapress.com
844-682-1282

Because of the dynamic nature of the Internet, any web addresses or links contained in this book may have changed since publication and may no longer be valid. The views expressed in this work are solely those of the author and do not necessarily reflect the views of the publisher, and the publisher hereby disclaims any responsibility for them.

The author of this book does not dispense medical advice or prescribe the use of any technique as a form of treatment for physical, emotional, or medical problems without the advice of a physician, either directly or indirectly. The intent of the author is only to offer information of a general nature to help you in your quest for emotional and spiritual well-being. In the event you use any of the information in this book for yourself, which is your constitutional right, the author and the publisher assume no responsibility for your actions.

Any people depicted in stock imagery provided by Getty Images are models, and such images are being used for illustrative purposes only.
Certain stock imagery © Getty Images.

Print information available on the last page.

ISBN: 979-8-7652-4229-2 (sc)
ISBN: 979-8-7652-4230-8 (hc)
ISBN: 979-8-7652-4228-5 (e)

Library of Congress Control Number: 2023914761

Balboa Press rev. date: 08/22/2023

Dedicated to: my Great Source for all the wisdom given; the message and words typed for this writing; thank you, Father/Mother God, Brother and Lord Jesus, and my All One Spirit.

To: Unity Worldwide Ministry, for spreading the love and manifestation of the Filmore's vision.

To: Unity of Pensacola, Florida, with the amazing Reverend Jamie Sanders for the aid of helping us to think outside of ourselves; for the awareness check-ins; and to strive to be our highest and truest selves. Thank you for your weekly words, Reverend Jamie.

Acknowledgment to: All the efforts and ability to develop this writing to Balboa Press Publishing. For all those who laid their eyes upon the manuscript; aided in tweaking; visualized the cover: understood the concept and aided in the writing to come to existence.

To: Sincere appreciation for educational providers who assist in identifying some students' learning differences.

To: The fourth-grade teacher: for identifying this person when they struggled with reading and writing. You helped them with a team of others, their parents, and a sibling for continued support at home. This person overcompensated for the differences and gained great belief in themselves to accomplish greatness when one puts their mind toward the issue. Thank you!

CHAPTER 1

Ten-year-old Aunewu stood in disbelief as he looked over the vast terrain of his homeland in Africa. He was overwhelmed with anxiety and awe at the same moment. Aunewu wondered why he was chosen and gifted with this vision and words. The World seemed upside down to him. A global pandemic, territorial wars, famine, climate change, an array of elders with their words of the World at change, and animal extinction, let alone his own family's destitution of their animal's livelihood. The World seemed impossible to fathom even at his young age, but he understood. Yet he had this vision and these words—why? What was he supposed to do as a youth in his society with such a message?

Aunewu gathered his staff, herd canines, and water and began to lead his herd back toward the paddock. He knew this message was of utmost importance, yet how would he present the information, and who was to believe him? When the livestock entrusted to his care was secured, he knew he had to speak up. With courage and determination, Aunewu began a short journey on foot to the respected elders' daily gathering place. His trusty canines went with him along the way. Aunewu glanced over at the canines and the vast terrain around him. His home was here, his family, his kinship to friends, livestock, and gardens of families he knew so well. Did the vision mean he would have to travel outside the territory? The anxiety began to well upon him again. Aunewu attempted to shake the dread, the thoughts, and the overwhelming feeling of wanting to run free from anxiety.

He arrived at the gathering place, and Aunewu stood silent as he knew disruption to the elders speaking was not permissible. An elder spotted Aunewu and squinted with one eye. Aunewu began to tremble. The elder then smiled and, in their native tongue, said for Aunewu to approach the group. One person standing along a side wall straightened his back from the wall, terror stretched across the face of Aunewu's father, Augustin. Aunewu felt as though his legs were not part of his body when his shoulders launched him forward, and his legs had to catch him from falling. The elder who spoke to Aunewu was Simounte, a great- grandelder to his family whose age was over one hundred years. Aunewu found his bearings and walked past his father to stand nearby Simounte. The elders were in disbelief that the young boy was not tending to the family's livestock as required, and murmurs were heard. Simounte appeared to understand the boy's intention. With the thump of the staff in his hand, the elders quieted. Simounte gave a hardy gesture that all was well; the boy had received a message.

Aunewu stood in disbelief. How did this one elder know, understand, and have no fear? Simounte gestured to the boy with a reassured smile, and the nerves Aunewu felt welling inside him seemed to dissipate. Simounte granted the boy a chance to speak, but Aunewu was hesitant. With a glance toward his father, who stood with a discerning look upon his face, he then glanced at Simounte. In the elder, he saw a calmness that reassured him. With what seemed to be no saliva in his mouth or voice in his throat, Aunewu stumbled with words in desperation to explain why he had entered the gathering. As the words began to tumble from his lips, he gained confidence with the reassured look upon the elders' faces. His backbone began to strengthen, his legs stopped quivering, and the hair standing on end throughout his body relaxed. Aunewu offered what he had experienced.

The vision was revealed that the World could be changed. The resolution was in the citizens of the World's hands. How could this be managed, as the World was a huge planet? The vision revealed the intent of the citizens to gather as one force. To complement the efforts, the Ascended

Masters would be aiding. A select few of the citizens around the World would receive the same vision, the same message. Which of these citizens would this be? Only the ones appointed from the spirits with like-minded thoughts, consciousness, actions, and deliberate intention. The group of elders remained still, almost unfazed by this revolution. Murmurs had begun slowly and quietly among the younger men in attendance. Upon the signal from Simounte, an elder to his right rose, positioned himself alongside Simounte, and aided him to his feet. Simounte walked with aid toward Aunewu and placed his hands upon Anuewu's shoulders as he gave a tight squeeze. Simounte turned toward the others gathered and, in their native tongue, recited the holiest of all words spoken: Amen.

Augustin was astonished by what he had heard his son recite for the vision and words given to him as a message. What was a father to do with a son such as this boy? Surely Aunewu made the whole event up in his head, and Simounte seemed as though to be honoring the boy. Simounte gestured for his staff; upon placement into his hand, he gestured for Augustin to come close to him. Augustin seemed frozen, unable to move his body toward the elder he gave respect. Slowly Augustin's muscles understood what his brain appointed and moved toward Simounte.

Feeling in a daze, Augustin realized the elder held his son in high regard. With the stomp of Simounte's staff, the other elders began to rise and form an impenetrable circle around the three men. The circle symbolized unity within the people's tribe. A validation that stood for: "Let no person penetrate and cause harm." Augustin had seen this only once during his lifetime. A tribal person returned from a journey with a message for a group of elders. The person was honored with a feast and night of rest prior to their departure. Would this be the same for his son, was his son to leave the land known as his home, his family, his tribe of like-minded people?

With another gesture of Simounte's hand, the group broke the circle and slowly left the gathering area. The three of them stood together. Aunewu, unsure of his place, now lowered his eyes toward the ground. Simounte smiled a large grin, placed his finger upon the boy's chin, and tilted Aunewu's head toward his gaze. Simounte gestured all three should be seated. With aid from Augustin, Simounte was lowered toward a pile of pillows. Aunewu knew to kneel and bow before his great-grandelder.

With a laugh, Simounte stated to Aunewu that it was not he granted such a grand vision and honorable words. Yet, it was he who was in awe of Aunewu and wished he was of the sound body to kneel and bow before Aunewu.

Both Augustin and Aunewu were astonished. The pair did not realize the volume in which this vision and words bestowed upon Aunewu. Simounte gestured first for Augustin to voice his concerns. Since nothing of this size had ever taken place for Aunewu, Augustin was mystified by what this meant for his son. Simounte gestured toward Aunewu to voice his concerns. Aunewu stammered out slowly the words. Does this mean he has to leave his home, his family, the family's animals, and his friends? Leave his territory, which he was entrusted to love, honor, and aid in its growth with nutrients for the inhabitants.

With a gentle tussle of Aunewu's hair from Simounte, as the boy's eyes bore a hole into the ground of the gathering area, Simounte chuckled. He told them both he had never received such a message and that the ground they were about to walk upon would be new ground. Simounte made no promises of Aunewu not having to leave his homeland, yet if Aunewu was requested, Simounte would send the boy with his blessings and protection. The volume of this vision and words could prompt such a journey for the boy. However, with reassuring words, Simounte stated the changes in the World would not happen overnight. Simounte explained he had seen an earlier tribal person leave the territory, yet this was a necessary movement for steps toward the continued independence of the tribe. The vision and words bestowed upon Aunewu were of a different velocity, and he also was unsure of the outcome. Now, Simounte held Aunewu in utmost respect and would support Aunewu concerning the matter.

2

Thirty-two-year-old Eusia felt the rush of cool breeze across her body as she gazed, astonished by what she had seen for a vision. Eusia was accustomed to her routine of daily life in her village in Asia. Scrubbing the clothing clean for her family and nearby relatives and elders in the community. She stood and wondered why such a vision and words were bestowed onto her and what she was to do with the information. Eusia gathered the clothing, glanced toward the others at the river, and mustered her body to connect with her brain. Her conscious connected the parts, and she found herself walking toward the women as they cleaned clothing along the riverside. She questioned them whether they had experienced the same. None of the other women had experienced the same, which left Eusia dismayed. She gathered herself and, with a clear and determined mind, began the short journey to her home.

She arrived home, and Eusia found her spouse, Rundda, as he cleaned the fish caught during his daily responsibilities to offer food for the family and village. She prepared the clothing on the line to dry and recited the information from the vision and words received. The Holy Ones above them had entrusted her with the information not to keep to herself and ponder but to spread an undeniable message to all others. Rundda at once set aside the fish and his cleaning knife, astounded by these words from his spouse. Rundda moved toward Eusia in haste. Exactly what had taken place? Why was she so confident with the information she had received? Rundda placed his hand upon Eusia's shoulder, and as she turned, he saw a calm and radiant peace about her. Their eyes met, and Rundda knelt on his knees and bowed toward his beloved spouse, who stood in front of him. Eusia was taken back by the gesture while she reached toward Rundda's shoulders.

Rundda's head remained in a downward position as she knelt beside him. Eusia placed her hands on his head and gently lifted. Their eyes met again. Rundda stated he felt in awe to be in such a presence and that he would gather the village elders. Eusia smiled and said she was the same person he always knew and loved; nothing about the message had changed their feelings for one another.

Rundda gathered himself, rose to his feet, and found himself again in movement beyond his comprehension. He had the mission to gather the elder village people to hear of this message. He only knew the message was for the elders to hear, to react, to put into place the next step for him and his spouse to embark. With nervous apprehension yet excitement, Rundda mustered the strength to gather the elders and other village onlookers in the village center. Almost as if telepathic, Eusia appeared as the last remaining elders gathered and were assisted to awaiting woven chairs. No apprehension stood between Runnda and Eusia as the radiant glow continued to surround her as she approached the center. Rundda joined his spouse in the center, anxious only about what the elders and others would hear, think, and their reactions. All leaned in towards the couple to hear the words Eusia was to speak.

As the same with Aunewu, the message was clear: the World could change with the integrated efforts of the citizens. The Ascended Masters were to aid the chosen few citizens with their knowledge and ability to make the transition seamless. What exactly did this pertain to; how would this come to be; who, within the village, would receive a message? So much information was lacking, yet the elders understood. Such information and action were depicted through the ages. They were in awe and reassured. Eusia stood in confidence while Rundda realized he needed to hold tightly to her hand. She felt the warmth and yet concern radiating from his touch. Eusia turned toward her spouse and, with a warm smile, reached toward him for an embrace. The elders in the village knew the magnitude of the message and were not astonished by the choice of the person. They knew the couple stood strong together, and no fear would reach any of them with the words the eldest had for the couple. Only a few individuals throughout the villagers had been bestowed such messages.

The eldest, Cambi, spoke with vigor and cheer. The couple was to prepare to embark on a journey to a destination unknown at the present time. However, Cambi knew more information was to follow through messages. The villagers began a slow and quiet whisper in the center. Eusia's raised her face and arms toward the sky, and all present recited the holiest of all words known to them: ATHEM, meant as Amen.

3

Seventy-two-year-old Warec felt like he had woken from a dream state as he reclined in his chair in Europe. He realized his cup of tea was to one side of his left hand, the book he was reading lay in his lap, and his body felt heavy. Confusion set into his brain as he grappled with the notion that what he had seen was only from a dream. Indeed, the vision and words he had seen and heard were only that from a dream state. But, to his scientific mind, what else could this have been? Why on Earth would he have been subject to such a ludicrous vision, and the words, the words they sounded so clear, so purposeful—what was the meaning to all he had encountered.

Warec gathered his bearings, picked up the book from his lap, snapped it closed, repositioned his cup on the side table, and began to rise from the chair. Warec stated out load "Whoever these so-called Ascended Masters were and whatever they needed to spread for information, they would have to do more convincing than what appeared to be a dream!" His brain connected with his muscles, and he found himself in motion toward his kitchen to make a fresh cup of tea and for a towel to pick up the tea on his floor.

4

Forty-nine-year-old Mabo stood not shocked at the vision and words he had received on the temple rooftop where he was the minister in South America. On the contrary, he was in awe of the splendor and beauty he had encountered. Mabo had known of the coming for quite some time, and although he wanted to shout from the temple rooftop, he refrained. Instead, he gathered the disciple books he had for study and the coming sermon he had prepared. Now Mabo would prep a different service on behalf of the upcoming encounter for the people of this vast and protected place.

The congregation of local people greeted Mabo as he descended from the rooftop. With a generous smile and a bit more pep in his step, he waved to those as they did chores for themselves, family members, and others in the area. He walked in wonder as he reflected on how beautiful and giving these people were in the land, peaceful and fulfilled; it was not a wonder they were to bring forth a wonderful message and era.

At his home, Mabo greeted his spouse, Tiao. She was a wonderful woman, he thought to himself, gifted to have her strength in his life. With a warm smile, embrace, and kindness in their eyes, Tiao knew something was new for her spouse. Wild wonder entered her thoughts. The peace and glow that encircled her spouse was radiant. She prepped the staples of their meal and offered a prayer before consumption. Mabo washed his hands, bent over the hot boiling pot over the open fire, and waved his hands upward to inhale the aroma. Then, with generous smiles at each other, they both sat to eat.

Tiao could no longer contain herself and burst with excitement at what her spouse had experienced with questions. Mabo told all he had experienced and announced they would prepare their home for visitors from afar. She beamed eagerly and said they would need aid for their home, the nearby property, barns, food, and animals. Tiao was so excited that she jumped from her seat, throwing her arms from one side of the room to the other. Finally, Mabo stood, moved toward Tiao wrapped her in his arms and said all was well. The villagers would take steps to complete the task. They would not complete all the efforts themselves.

5

Twenty-seven-year-old Samuel in Australia, injected the endangered species—Gilbert Potoroo named Zeal, with his daily dose of vitamins. Samuel repositioned the mineral block in Zeal's enclosure and stood up. He smiled at the progress Zeal had made since his arrival at the zoo. Samuel released Zeal to gain mobility and turned to exit the enclosure. He felt a warmth across his body as he began to lose his balance and felt himself tumble toward the Earth. He braced himself for the blow as his body fell. Then, in a dizzy spin of his body his waist turned and he found himself upright.

For several moments he stood as if time had stopped. Then, he saw a vision and heard exact words said out loud. Samuel snapped back to the present as he tried to regain his bearings. He wondered if others near the enclosure had seen the same vision and had heard the words. After Samuel exited the enclosure, he questioned others about the words and vision he had seen and heard. None had experienced the same, and most appeared concerned that Samuel had experienced heat exhaustion or other symptoms. Samuel laughed and shrugged off the concern of others. He gathered his homeopathic items and notebook and turned toward his office.

Samuel felt disorientated from the experience. After entering the office, he grabbed his water bottle and sat for a long while. Samuel knew his work as a zoologist/ herbologist was valued, and his written word on the internet aided in other zoos and veterinary offices. He had experienced several new aspirations in his short stint at the zoo. Samuel valued the veterinarians and fellow zoologists for their knowledge and skills. Why had he been the one to experience the words and vision? After all, the others were more experienced and mature than he; how could he describe the information that was so valuable to others—to be taken seriously? Certainly, someone else in the area had experienced the same. He convinced himself to approach the others with more scientific evidence to present the information.

6

Fifty-seven-year-old Katerina stood on the vast tundra of Antarctica laid out before her. She steadied herself after the experience she had received with undeniable words and a vision. For the Geophysicist and renowned scientist, she felt as cold as the weather could be during winter on this continent, yet it was summertime in the hemisphere. Katerina was in the part of the World where few others resided. The only others gathered were scientists, mathematicians, astrologists, and locals living in the area seasonally. Why, of all people, had she experienced such a phenomenon? What exactly did this mean for others gathered here? For the World?

Katerina struggled to gather her bearings, to pack her apparatus and supplies into her backpack. To connect her body with her brain to even gain mobility. She needed to speak to someone—anyone about the experience. She wanted to know if anyone experienced the same. In the wonder of all the land around her, she paused, breathed a deep breath and exhaled slowly. She realized the vision was so vivid, so beautiful, so direct. The Earth's land healed, the animals returned, and the fowl traveled without ailment with such grace and ease. The atmospheric conditions were clear and crisp, with no pollution detected within her senses.

How on Earth could this ever be possible? For all her years, her research, and her networking among some of Earth's most remarkable minds, was this vision and words probable? Katerina felt an impressive peace, awareness, and stillness within her, and she welled up with anticipation of the prospect. Her inner self became giddy; her mind raced with all the admiration of the ones who called themselves the Ascended Masters who divulged such information to her. Had not she and fellow scientists, mathematicians, astrologists, and the locals all wondered when the Earth would or could be changed?

She let out a joyous sigh and laugh as she realized the Masters gave the notion, vision, and information; the time was upon them, and the time was now. What an exalting thought, what joy the World would feel and the transformation that would take place. The question was how? Katerina knew the information. The feeling of such happiness, her understanding, could not be withheld. Then she set out on the vast land before her to join Suri, the one person on the continent who would not think she had gone mad after so many months of being there.

7

Nineteen-year-old Quiatua sat mesmerized in her yoga position and looked out of her North American tree house. What on Earth had she just experienced? It seemed like a trance state with a clear and intentional vision. The words she heard were precise and undeniable. From early childhood, she had always experienced communication with her Spirit Guide, Azna, and had knowledge of Ascended Masters. Yet, these Ascended Masters spoke directly to her as they explained the vision.

During her lifetime, Quiatua had been guided through Azna to study the growing cycles of the ecological systems, astronomy, astrology, physical form, and matter. For anything she had an interest in, Azna was there, cheering her on to study. Her Guide was her most prominent advocate. When she spotted the circular tree form in the forest and acknowledged out loud where she chose to build her tree house, Azna equipped her with experts in the local area. Quiauta had to stretch her mind and grasp mathematics, science, suspension, and anything to achieve her goal. She studied the human body, biophysics, and medicine. Anything she put her mind toward Azna had always aided.

Quiatua breathed deeply and asked, as always, Azna for aid. In a moment, Azna presented the situation and explained it. Yes, Quiatua was one of the few selected to initiate the transition of the World toward resurrection. She would experience precisely as Azna had communicated in this lifetime—the revival of the planet, the air, the animals, the plants, the trees—everything! What a wonder the people here on this planet would experience!

Taken back for the moment, Quiatua gathered her consciousness, convinced her brain to connect with her muscles and stood upright. She marveled as her legs carried her toward her balcony. She smiled wide, laughed hard, stood shaking, and cried deeply. Finally, something she had longed for in her life had begun. Her cries were complete bliss. The time had come, the time was now, and she was smack dab in the center of the incredible journey; she could not wait to know what came next.

CHAPTER 2

Omarya oversaw the council of Ascended Masters, and with clear intention, he sent out the message telepathically for all those Masters regarding the Bridge to assemble. He was to aid these Masters in the orientation of the chosen humans. However, he needed first knowledge of each human and why the Master chose such a human. As he decided the area was open for further interaction from the Masters, Dyne was eager to share his information about the human he chose. With a reason behind the choice, he signaled his readiness.

Dyne began telepathically to all present. Then he introduced the others with visualization to Aunewu; his parents; family; village, and the beauty of his national land. The animals, which were in abundance, roamed free, the skies filled with clear air and fowl, and the water ran fresh and clean. The Masters detected only a small amount of pollution in the area, and the soil flourished with abundant growth of plants, trees, and various vegetation of flowers and herbs.

Dyne appointed he chose Aunewu for his genuine kindness to all that was around him. Aunewu took nothing of his daily existence for granted. He was in awe of the love felt by his parents, siblings, elders, village people, animals, plants, and the herbs gathered for therapeutic purposes. Daily, Aunewu gave the love he received in return, especially to the Earth. He had great respect for Mother Earth and wanted Her to heal. The skies and air to be cleaner, the animals to gain in numbers, and the soil to continue flourishing for the village.

The Ascended Masters marveled at the age of Aunewu and knew that the generation of the youth had every need to be involved. To have a child informed of the transition and for other children to grasp the ideals was very important. One Master questioned Dyne of Augustin, father of Aunewu, and his willingness to accept his son to undertake such a significant task. Dyne, unflustered by the question, sent loving thoughts to the others. These loving thoughts were the thought and feeling Augustin carried for Aunewu. Omarya projected thoughts of the village people and their support for father and son. Without a doubt, Dyne sent thoughts of knowing the people would give full support.

Well pleased with the selection, Formli chose to visualize her choice. Mabo was a male spiritual leader whose deep commitment to Mother Earth resonated with his village people. His love for his spouse, children, siblings, elders, animals, and plant life was enormous. Mabo realized he would not be the man he was without their support. Daily his joy was seen; he knew their worth, which brought him peace and vibrated outward to them—regarded as a high holy man with direct communication in the spirit world in the surrounding area.

Formli projected the thoughts to the others for Mabo and his spouse. The Ascended Masters were in awe of the respect others gave them both. The village region was ideal for gathering numerous humans to assemble. The area to be prepared for the assembly did not go unacknowledged by the Masters. The number of humans sent to assist would be grand. Formli received the thought of appreciation for her choice and felt honored to present the outstanding human, Mabo, and others who would help him.

Next to share his readiness was Yellow, who projected the thoughts of Warec. Omarya and the other Masters were stunned with wonder. With visualization, Yellow launched the first encounter with Warec. Some Masters projected concern about Warec's skepticism. However, where else was there a time without a doubt in human history and their interaction? Yellow selected the convincing of Warec would be an incredible journey and blissful event as not all humans were cooperative. Therefore, Warec would exemplify by example, knowing other skeptics would follow.

Yallow sent out his thoughts to the others and signaled. The World needed Warec's intricate part of his intelligence to envision the Earth's transformation. Warec was a pharmaceutical physician who also studied a great deal in the natural approach to treatment. Human societies would need his and the other's chosen abilities in the upcoming transition. A silence of telepathic thought overcame the group, and Omarya agreed, un-waivered by the silence. Omarya understood the generation to inherit the Earth was each generation present, and the next generation to come needed the benefit of Warec's knowledge.

Next with excitement was Baou. She projected her visualization of Quiatua, the minimalistic dweller with a massive appetite for study and knowledge. The spontaneity of Quiatua turned all Ascended Master's attention to her spirit and depth, the necessity to explore all things given to her with her Spirit Guide Azna to consult. Moreover, her sweetness made other living beings gravitate toward her. The kindness she bestowed on the land, animals, sky, and earth was undeniable.

Yet concern grew when Quiatua had only a little other human interaction. Could such a human interact with other humans to master the transition? Where was Quiatua's support system, as she appeared to have lived alone? Baou sent thoughts to the other Masters, yes Quiatua was born of parents who were free- willed in their convection of—the World is all you need, live within your means, and you shall always have abundance. But unfortunately, Quiatua lost her parents and two siblings as a young teenager due to a dwelling fire.

She was unharmed as she had slept outside on her tree platform, unaware of the fire, until the smell of smoke reached her senses. In fright, Quiatua was awoken and climbed from her platform, ran toward the dwelling only to find it engulfed in flame. Quiatua was assured by Azna her family had felt no pain, and they had made the pack before their arrival on Earth to perish together. Quiatua was the only survivor. In another lifetime, she had died from a dwelling fire. Since the land was where she was familiar, she stayed and made do with what the Earth offered.

As for why Baou chose Quiatua, she was familiar with living in abundance with the Earth. She projected to the other Masters all that was there for others to learn from Quiatua, who was like some other humans chosen, to live within their means. Other humans would receive help from her experience and the gift of sharing her knowledge. The adjustment to Quiatua would suit her to learn about human interaction. Baou and Azna had her covered; she would not walk alone. Others would receive help from the interaction with her as well.

Peluan visualized his chosen human next. Eusia with her spouse, Rundda, were from a like-minded village who both held within their essence, healing. The holistic healers were paramount throughout the transition, and he was honored to present them. Eusia had known since her choice of life she would inhabit an area that needed her healing and had selected her partner, Rundda, in earlier lifetimes. Once as her all-so-wise grandfather, once as her minister, once as a physician to uncurable disease as she needed to experience the sensation, and as her soulmate in this lifetime.

The Ascended Masters were astounded by the connection between the couple and well pleased with the choice. For such a couple to leave the village and travel a great distance, would not the village lack healers? Would some not have a proper diagnosis of their ailments? Without further delay, Peluan visualized all humans in the village that gained extraordinary knowledge from the couple as they spread their life mission to others. They shared the Reiki study and teachings from the great experts before them for several lifetimes shared. The choice was foreseeable as the humans around the World who knew of the relief Reiki, massage, herbal and vegetation digestion, as well as salve and ointments use, would gravitate toward them.

With their knowledge of health and the other humans chosen, the team began to form and agreed upon from the Masters. As for Rundda, he was an advanced thinker in his village. His dwelling lifestyle showed using the Earth to its fullest extent. Harnessing wind, solar, and water resources was always considered throughout the village's expansion. Wastewater and sewage were a specialty with him, the transition of the Earth would go back to the basics—the Earth needed the reset.

With relief, Luna presented in visualization her chosen human, Samuel—the fine zoologist who studied and practiced herbology for himself and the animals under his care. Occasionally, the coworkers asked him for aid with aliments for themselves and the animals in their care. With triumphant pleasure, Luna shared her thoughts and highlighted

Samuel's kindness and light yet firm touch when needed he had with the animals and other humans.

The Masters welcomed these kind actions of Samuel as they had concerns from the beginning of all animals on Earth and the transition. All humans could benefit from the example Samuel, fellow zoologists, veterinarians, marine biologists, avian scientists, volunteers, and trainers would have upon animals as cruel and harsh lifetimes for animals would be no longer. The World respected Samuel's longing to study and gain much knowledge from his coworkers and others. With such a knowledge base with this caring human, others could only follow his steps. The World respected Samuel's expertise and talents for his insight and instinct.

The extraordinary gift was Samuel's further study, research, and writings of herbal remedies for animals. Samuel's herbal knowledge could only benefit others who followed the same path. The sharing of the knowledge they had obtained would be well-balanced and appreciated by Samuel. He was extraordinary man with insights into animals, humans, and all living things on Earth. The extinction of the World's animals was of concern, and Luna agreed Samuel would collaborate well with other humans and the animals would flourish in his care and multiply.

Koyro waited to present the Masters with his choice of Katerina, knowing the others would be in awe. He visualized the present dwelling place of Katerina and her life partner Suri. The Masters felt a blast of air hit the assembly, and some felt lighter. Antarctica's air was less polluted, and they appreciated the locale choice. The skies burned a crimson shade before sunset, and the Masters took in the beauty of the land and the two women as they spoke outside the dome dwelling.

Whales, walruses, and fowl flocked into the area by the numbers, and the Masters admired the courage of the women to dwell within this remote area. Suri was a woman who had a family lineage from New Zealand with a position of hierarchy. She needed to be herself and not fold to her parent's place in the line. Suri had studied at great scholastic colleges for her advancement in mathematics. While on safari in Africa, Katerina and Suri met when researching the area under a doctoral dissertation. The women revealed their truth and could not deny their love for one another. The diversity of the interracial, same-gender couple pleased the Masters as they knew inclusion was a big part of Earth's transition.

With Katerina and Suri's knowledge, skills, and continuous yearning to develop more, they were an outstanding choice for the transition, and the Masters agreed enthusiastically. Suri would win over people with her genuine human side, while Katerina would light the skies with her generous self to all others, animals, and the Earth itself. They both supported the energy to be productive assets to the formed team. Koyro visualized the couple as they shared their findings daily and how much they relied upon each other to absorb all the Artic land offered. He offered to the Masters that the World respected their knowledge and was ecstatic when the Masters agreed to his choice.

CHAPTER 3

Thoughts filled the assembly with a flurry. Omarya felt pleasure for the hay day that unfolded among the Ascended Masters. During the Earth's history, other grand resets involved all humans. Yes, there had been floods, famine, war and its destructive devices, earthquakes, sea rising, lakes drying, wildfires, diseases to animal kingdoms and humans, the plant and tree life. Yet, this reset would involve the humans gathering and using their talents, skills, and knowledge with guidance from the Ascended Masters, Spirit Guides, and the Great Source, and with all the messengers sent before. Omarya knew the undertaking was vast, while humans collaborating with like-minded humans would rapidly expand the globe.

All spiritual belief systems throughout the World would gather as one. Peace would begin to shine its light and way to those even in the remote areas, and positive thoughts would penetrate the more oppressed regions and the skeptics alike. He knew now was the time to introduce the great messenger—Akaham, from the Source. The Masters would gain from Akaham the knowledge needed to transpire for the Earth and its inhabitants for the greater good of all. Akaham had a knack for making all feel heard with their thoughts. He would settle the commotion once he entered the assembly.

Omarya generated the light sounds of the rhythmic flutes, the Blessed Ones began a chorus, and a soft trumpet started filling the area. Once he was pleased the chaos had settled to a quiet atmosphere; he focused on a presence that entered the assembly. The Masters fell in complete silence with their thoughts. Omarya took in the magnitude of the event which unfolded before them all. Then, with great honor, he projected his thoughts to the others as he introduced Akaham to all those who had gathered.

Akaham projected his form to the others in the middle of all their thoughts, which assumed space magnificently. Next to Akaham, a feminine entity began to appear from his thoughts. Akaham introduced the Masters to the entity; his feminine equal appointed from the Great Source as Maik. He projected they would oversee the more in-depth aspects the Great Source was to divulge upon all humankind. It was not their duty to correct the Masters and their choice of the humans they had inspired to bring through Earth's transition: but to explain the process. With a significant pause in the energy level, the Masters settled their thoughts, for the selections had been a long process.

Maik projected her thoughts out to all who had gathered. She appreciated that humans from each continent were chosen and this pleased the Great Source. The beginning of the transition would be outstanding for all generations on Earth to see. Each human chosen would begin an incredible journey toward the designated area of Mabo's region.

Formli, Mabo's Ascended Master, would soon begin projecting thoughts to the villagers of the great honor bestowed upon them. Others would gather, and the area would be transformed with great care and preparation. To allow for many humans who would follow once the transition began. She projected the Masters should not concern themselves with the preparation, yet concentrate their energy on the humans they had chosen and prepare them for the journey.

Akaham projected his thoughts of how humans with diseases, mobile disabilities, compromised health issues, and any known human ailments would begin to be lifted Worldwide. What a great accomplishment that this would be done upon all of Earth. Only the Great Source could and would make this happen, but why? Were humans not to experience these ailments to grow as spiritual entities and must repeat the same or likewise with their loved ones? After all, was this not the reason for human life on Earth, that their experiences were transferred to Great Source so they could also experience? Akaham knew the thoughts would come, and the commotion soon began.

With a gesture from Akaham's projected form, the attention of all assembled was directed toward an area. A cloud formed, and projections from the Great Source were seen. Those with ailments could not experience the actual transformation, and the Source considered this. They wanted the generations of the World to begin the transition with whole bodies and minds. Projecting this, they thought the soul of humans would also start to follow. Simple enough to be expected. However, humans were known to have minds of their own, spiritual beliefs of their own, and were creatures of habit, usually. What was going to be the actual outcome of the transition after all? Would this not hinder the aspirations of the Great Source?

One Ascended Master projected his thought in a question form. So much negative, harmful, and devastation had been bestowed upon humankind by some humans. What would become of those who dispelled the conditions onto others? Ah, with great anticipation, Akaham knew the question would come. Those who had dispelled such on others, the animal kingdom, the environment, etc., and had not come to terms with their decisions to follow their negative ways or that of others, would fall asleep at one time or another and never wake up. What, project all that again? Yes, as in pass away without regard to firming up their affairs, their redemption for their actions, or otherwise.

After all, had they not experienced what they came to experience? The Masters' thoughts flooded the assembly. With a calming gesture, Omarya directed his thoughts to still the Masters' ideas into order. Akaham projected to the cloud, as the Source had considered all this. The Source had their share of lives reincarnating to experience being an assailant or victim. The time had ended— enough of any thoughts about this and for Akaham to continue.

Maik projected her thoughts toward the cloud. Visualization appeared of wounded animals, plant life, humans, and all living beings as the healing of the World spread. Thoughts flooded the assembly with positive energy. Isn't this what the Masters yearned for generation after generation of human life on Earth? Indeed, the Masters began to visualize the Earth as a whole. The places they lived prior themselves, the worry, the frustration, the joy, the beauty which at times were ripped from their lifetime. They had achieved great experiences in their lifetimes engineered for their growth, to leave behind having to reincarnate any further.

As Ascended Masters, they had to take on many responsibilities life after lifetime to gain their experiences and atone. They had expelled great energy for generations to humankind so as not to live so many lifetimes making their mistakes. At times this seemed as though it fell upon the deaf minds of humanity. The time had come for this to begin to change. Their energy efforts had been well- spent after all this time. The need for more understanding of this took Akaham and Maik aback. The Great Source projected on the cloud to them both, and all assembled, the greatest gift to humankind was that they were never alone. All humanity was to come to know this soon enough, not just the chosen humans but all humans.

The Blessed Ones chorus began softly, the trumpet chimed in softly, and the flutes began a harmony with all. Maik and Akaham readjusted their energy and continued. If ailments were dissipated, what would become of the physicians, pharmacists, biologists, and all those who studied medicine and science. These humans who followed a path of these fields would chime in with those who studied, ate, and breathed life into the herbology, medicinal intuition of plants, water, and all-natural alternatives for the betterment of all Earth's inhabitants. Such a grand culmination together would begin between the fields. The due cause of so many ailments began with the pollution of the Earth and its living inhabitants being subject. The only need for medicine would be replaced with natural alternatives, as it was meant in Earth's beginning.

Would this mean pollution of the Earth would dissolve, as some Masters projected? When the Great Source resets the Earth, then yes, humankind could only begin to heal, when the Earth was healed. What a concept to behold, all pollution from the Earth to be lifted and thrown into the most bottomless black hole of the universe. The Master's energy shifted to the reality on hand; all would resume being well. For Great Source to have faith in humankind not to destroy the Earth but to aid in the transition for betterment; they were inspired.

Several Masters projected their thoughts out to the assembled. What would take place with the political environment of the Earth? Some areas vibrated light and positivity while others seemed gray, dark in nature—so much negativity. How would this be able to be changed and stabilized from the Source in the future? A brilliant light illuminated the cloud; such power and grace filled the assembly. The Masters and all in attendance were in awe. The Source projected as the same with one spiritual belief system spreading Worldwide. The same would be of the stabilized political environments. With one belief system, where would the unrest come from in the political climate? All would unfold into one another, the Source projected.

It sounded simple enough, yet how would humankind seriously begin all these things toward transition? Fair enough, how about the Source begin with dispelling negative energy, healing the humans, healing the animal kingdom, healing the atmosphere, and witness the transformation spread across the Earth? The cloud dissipated instantaneously as Maik and Akaham's energy began to fade. But wait, what had taken place, there was so much uncertainty, so much not explained!

Without further delay, Omarya projected thoughts toward the assembled. More informational projections would come as the Great Source manifested them toward the Masters, Guides, and all messengers sent before. Patience was a virtue, Omarya reminded all assembled. Each assembled had mastered patience, which was part of the process during their atonement—no need for further interaction as the assembly was dismissed. Omarya's energy began to fade. Rapid-fire thoughts were projected from the Ascended Masters; after all, the information granted to them—would rock the World!

Chapter 4

Mabo had finished his sermon and stood resilient in the congregational hall. The villagers began a faint hum of words, and soon the confusion resonated off the walls. Finally, Mabo's spouse, Tiao, stood and walked to her husband with a proud smile. She embraced his shoulders with both arms and planted a massive kiss on his forehead. She revealed a handmade ornament necklace and generously placed it over his head and shoulders, prepared and pinned an item directly over his heart. Mabo felt pride in his wife's intricate detail of the emblem, he embraced Tiao, and both knelt in front of the statue of the congregation's rendition of the Great Source.

The villagers fell silent in wonder. How did all the words Mabo said have any overall truth? Just as a slow murmur began, a cloud appeared. Then the villagers were astonished and fell silent. Mabo waved his hand upward and started a chant. Tiao joined the chant, and others began to chant. Soon soft drum sounds and flutes began to be heard. Finally, the cloud formed into Mabo's Ascended Master, Formli. With wild wonder, the congregation started slowly to kneel and bow their heads.

Formli, in her complete form, made a gesture over the congregation and bowed toward them with a broad smile. As she explained, she was honored to greet them all. She wondered at their resilience to the rest of the World and how true to their lifestyle they had become. Formli stated that water, land, animals, vegetation, fowl, air, and all living matters flourished because they cared for the Earth. Formli explained that other Ascended Masters had projected their thoughts to her; they were genuinely impressed and grateful to the people of this region. All the people of the area should feel pride in their accomplishments.

With a gesture from Mabo, all in attendance were to be seated on their cushions. Formli had projected that the task would be a vast undertaking and understood all efforts would be needed. Hence, the honor bestowed upon them from the Great Source. Mabo had presented to them to work together to prepare the region for the influx of others. While some villagers felt anxious about the endeavor, others were immediate to begin. However, as told by Formli, this needed to be orderly, and instruction would come through messenger transmissions from the Great Source.

2

Both women smiled at one another when the ship departed Antarctica toward Australia. Katerina and Suri had discussed their expected journey before the departure with the others. Although the other people present seemed skeptical, both women seemed unfazed, and more determination rose within them. They knew since their first contact through Koyro, Katerina's Ascended Master, to be a zoologist in Australia named Samuel. Suri presented the sentiment to Katerina of her need to visit her parents before the South American journey. Katerina appreciated the thought and agreed.

The women settled in for the ship's journey and listened to their selected music playlist. When Suri chose her favorite song, "Every Kind of People" by Robert Palmer, Katerina beamed. They spoke of their excitement with the journey. After all, a Geophysicist and Mathematician, where would their talents, education, and knowledge be best used for this transition? Why on Earth did they need to travel and meet this Samuel person?

So much excitement and both women were ecstatic that they did not have to experience the journey without each other. What new concepts, strategies, and experiences were they about to embark on together? The excitement boiled in each one of them, and laughter began. How many others were chosen? What would all these people have in common to signify a transition of the Earth? How was all this going to be managed with others involved? They knew that the Earth's evolution involved more inclusive thoughts. Did this mean they would be part of the genuine effort to manifest their desire for a unified acceptance among all people of the World? Both women settled in for the evening and began to drift off to sleep, then Koryo appeared.

3

Quiatua checked her tree house, water catchment and distribution system, solar power panel, and batteries, along with her handwritten notes. She had been instructed by Azna, her Spirit Guide, to bring the notes with her on the journey to South America. South America! The thoughts generated welled inside her once again. She was so excited she could barely sleep the past week. Through Azna, she had the opportunity to meet with her Ascended Master, Baou, telepathically over the past weeks. She knew the size of the transition better as time went on and why she was one of the chosen few.

Azna gave her all the support and knowledge for years. Finally, Quiatua was so excited she could not stand the thoughts any longer and stowed the notes in her bag. She grabbed her bags, pillow, and sweet teddy-bear stuffed animal as she closed and locked the door. She took a deep breath and then exhaled. She loaded all items except the bear onto the lift, grabbed the cord, and lowered the lift toward the ground. She held tight to the bear, giggled with glee, kissed the bear on the head, and descended the staircase. Bear was given to her as a child by her parents, he was the one mainstay in her life besides Azna, and he was not to miss this journey!

At the foot of the staircase, Baou, her Ascended Master, appeared in a mist, alone. Being alone without Azna struck Quiatua and made her uncomfortable and awkward. Sensing unease, Baou began to communicate telepathically. From this point forward, both she and Azna would guide her. First, she made a gesture with what appeared to be a staff from her form. Then, like what seemed to be the fairy tale Quiatua was inside, a horse, cart, and driver appeared. How could this be possible? Baou told her that the cart full of comfortable hay was for her travels. The driver and horse knew the direction of the journey.

Without further worry, Quiatua smiled broadly to Baou, gathered her bags from the lift, hoisted the lift, secured the cord, and threw her bags into the cart. She felt so secure in Baou's presence, with the horse so regal, and the driver had such a kind face and smile. She felt the curiosity building again when she climbed into the rear of the cart. She found comfort in the hay and settled in with her bear. As silly as she felt, she knew the bear was her grounding, her sounding board. Baou knew of her apprehension of others and what they would think of bear, she made a gesture again, and Quiatua understood. All was well, and the bear welcomed; after all, humans needed their sounding boards, didn't they?

With a gesture again, the horse moved forward as the driver, who seemed human enough yet, for some reason, angelic, made clicking sounds, and the horse's speed increased. Azna then appeared and knew of Quiatua's excitement, she communicated to her telepathically to rest, and dreams would come to her shortly. Dreams? How could this be? Quiatua hadn't dreamt, it seemed since before her parents and siblings had passed. However, she did not fight the sleep that descended upon her, as her vision began to fade like the mist with Baou and Azna, also evaporated.

4

Eusia and her spouse, Rundda, sat quietly at the international airport. The days and journey were long to this point. They both needed some peace. Rundda knew in only a few more days; his spouse would be inundated with new people and thoughts and consumed by all actions toward the World's transition. He would also be inside the commotion, yet Eusia, after all, had heard the words and seen the vision. Both had encountered Eusia's Ascended Master, Peluan, over the past weeks to prepare them for the journey to South America.

Rundda felt confident in their talents, belief systems, and knowledge. He also figured the emersion Eusia was to embark upon would also be overwhelming to her. Peluan projected thoughts that Eusia would not be alone in the journey. Like-minded humans with healing abilities would contribute to the efforts. However, he felt uneasy about the toll this would induce on his beloved. They had, for months, tried to conceive a child. Would all this be possible with what lay ahead? Sensing her spouse had drifted wildly away from the moment in thought, Eusia nudged Rundda back to the present.

An older gentleman settled in a chair across from the couple. The couple and gentleman exchanged glances, nodded toward one another, and broke eye contact. After some time, Rundda felt a relentless urge to converse with the man. When the words presented themselves and tumbled out of his mouth, Eusia was stunned. To her, Rundda was the last to speak to others, let alone a stranger. The man seemed annoyed with the sudden communication from this person seated across from him.

Warec had convinced himself since the weeks he had met with some entity known as Yallow, supposedly some Ascended Master or something, he'd better follow along with the plan. The plan placed him in the middle of an international airport with a foreign person wearing some regalia that Warec had never seen before. And this man had just abruptly spoken out loud to him. Yes, he was annoyed by the whole journey. Yet, Warec, for some reason, felt compelled to acknowledge the man and answer his question.

He made eye contact with the man and said he would travel to South America. Eusia smiled kindly, and Rundda sensed they might have been traveling to the same destination. Rundda spoke up to the man where their destination was also, South America and told the man he tried to understand why it mattered to him. Eusia smiled and spoke to both men. Yes, the unexplained feeling Rundda had was correct with his reservations. They were all to travel to the same destination for the same reason. Warec was stunned and did not honestly believe he would travel with other chosen people.

He tried to hide his discomfort, but this was unconvincing. Warec made eye contact with Eusia, who spoke gentle words to him. Words that had a purpose, meanings that solidified the entire past weeks. How could this be? He was beside himself, stood, and connected his brain with his legs to carry him toward the terminal window. Eusia glanced at Rundda with a confident look as she knew through her Master, Peluan, they would meet a man who would be skeptical of the experience. Peluan had communicated with her the extent of the encounter with this man, that he would be in disbelief, and then it would register to him: the transition was truly ahead for the World.

5

Aunewu stood on the deck of the massive ship when he and his father, Augustin, embarked on the incredible journey to a place called South America. He had seen his father offer to the villager after arrival to this place, from a small pouch, some bright material of some type. His father had explained to him the material was considered coins and their worth was immense. The village elders had given his father the pouch before their departure a few days ago. He thanked the villager and motioned a farewell gesture of safe travels to return to the village. Although they had traveled many miles through vast lands and towns and finally arrived at this place, Aunewu felt bored most of the trip.

Bewildered excitement read across Aunewu's face; his eyes lit from the anticipation as the sun above scourged down upon them. Augustin had told his son the journey across the sea would be longer than the trek across the land. He expected Aunewu to be polite, not to bother the workers or wander the ship. Aunewu knew from his encounters with Dyne, his Ascended Master, that his father's worry was great. Dyne had explained his father worried about rough seas or that Aunewu would venture too far with his upper body over the railing and fall into the churning sea below. There would be no explanation for his mother if this were the case scenario. Aunewu had promised Dyne he understood, and there would be no need for worry.

Aunewu stood fascinated by all taking place around him. The workers, their chatter, the commands they called out, their efforts ran 'like a fine-tuned machine.' When Aunewu showed concern to Dyne about ship travel, those were Dyne's words, in other words—to trust the process. Both Aunewu and Augustin were amazed by the rumble felt under their feet. The engines geared up when the ship pulled from the docking area. Augustin's body swayed to the left when the massive ship lurched forward. He grasped Aunewu's shoulder to steady himself and signaled the movement of the boat was magnificent yet needed to be respected. Neither of them had experienced such a sensation prior. He knew he had to ensure Aunewu was accounted for on the ship.

Just when he caught a glimpse of Aunewu's eager eyes, a young man approached them. The man said his name was Atony, and the captain had sent him to instruct them about safety, life jackets, the lifeboats, and off-limit areas of the ship. From there, the trio traveled around the deck and down below deck to their cabin. Atony told them they were both welcome to join the crew and captain at dinner in the galley once refreshed from their long journey over land. With unbridled excitement, Aunewu thanked Atony as he rushed past him and threw his body's weight onto the bunk. One bunk for him and one bunk for his father: his life was great, he thought to himself, and he was able to share the journey with his father—his best friend!

6

Sunset had fallen upon the zoo in Australia, and Samuel saw how beautiful the area had become. Although the day was full of hustle and bustle, the zoo became serene when dusk and dawn took place. Samuel stood at the foot of the exotic bird enclosure, fascinated by how they flew freely. However, he longed for all the animals to be truly free from captivity. He began to reflect on the experience when he glimpsed two women nearby the large cat exhibit.

Samuel was called to meet with a fellow zoologist at the exhibit. The two women stood in awe of the big cats and appeared to long for interaction with them. He side-stepped past them only to hear his name called a few steps past both women. His eyes glanced ahead of him and saw no one in the area. He turned at his waist, and his eyes contacted the women's eye contact. They seemed to know him from somewhere, but he could not place it if he knew them. Then he realized Luna, his Ascended Master, had communicated to him of the two women.

Without further delay, he strode toward them. Suri had extended her hand first to him. Samuel was amazed by her calm mannerism, while Katerina flashed him a knowing smile on her face. For a moment, it felt like time stood still for Samuel. Katerina and Suri waited for him to catch his breath and connect with his consciousness. When the realization came to Samuel, both women giggled like adolescents: after all, the three were in for a journey like nothing they had experienced prior. Samuel felt at once comfortable in their presence and initiated conversation.

A conversation as the three recalled what had occurred for the past weeks. Katerina was introduced to Koyro, while Samuel was introduced to Luna around the same time. Suri had prayed and meditated on the information obtained from Katerina in the beginning. She stated her Ascended Master, Gaiz, had affirmed she was to journey with her life partner without a doubt! Samuel marveled at the way all Ascended Masters knew so much of them and the journey they were to embark upon.

The women had said they met on safari and were mesmerized by the big cats in the exhibit. The three stood in astonishment at what the vision and words had depicted. The animals of the World ran free, no abused or neglected animals, and the air so pure and the water clean for all inhabitants. Katerina and Suri told Samuel about their career fields and they had arrived from Antarctica the day before. He felt small in comparison to them and their accomplishments. That was when their Ascended Masters appeared and corrected Samuel's feelings of inadequacies which surprised the women.

After all, were they not all chosen to use their skills, knowledge, and talents toward the transition? Samuel had replied sheepishly, yes, but he couldn't understand what he would contribute to all. Both women smiled, and he felt at ease. They explained Samuel would contribute significantly to the animals and the humans. How could he not? His care radiated around them. His aura was shining, as they said. Aura? What the heck were they saying?

Luna had projected her thoughts out to all present. The projection showed how Samuel was to aid others with their animals and how he would set so many free by explaining their misunderstood mannerisms from humans. That is when the women became delighted, took Samuel by the arms, and announced it was time for their behind-the-scenes zoo tour. Samuel consciously connected his brain with his legs and began to move forward. The trio glanced backward to see the mist dissipate that had appeared with their Ascended Masters. For some reason, Samuel felt connected to a sense of belonging for the first time since he had arrived in Australia.

The women had told Samuel they were to travel next to New Zealand to visit the family of Suri. Without further delay, they hugged Samuel and stated they would see him again in South America. South America, right? He had to organize his thoughts with designated people to charge the animals in his care. In addition, he had some personal matters to put in place. A long overdue telephone conversation with his parents was one of those matters. He had dreaded the thought; nevertheless, he knew he no longer would postpone. How would he begin to explain he was to leave for South America in two days, let alone—why?

CHAPTER 5

Quiatua had awoken well-rested and full of questions one day before arriving at her destination. She had grabbed bear tightly, swung her leg over the backboard of the driver's seat and seated herself next to the driver. She began to plunge into asking the driver for answers. Who was he? How far did he travel just for her sake? What was his name, what was the horse's name, and what did he do next after their arrival? She had wild wonder on her side and wanted to take advantage of the time. Just the two of them time, as she understood soon her whole life would change.

The driver had told her, he was a Spirit Guide, and like Azna, her Spirit Guide, he had the same abilities. His name was Saib, the horse was not named, but she was free to name him. From his vantage point, there was no travel to reach her that first encounter. Upon their arrival in South America and her introduction to the couple who awaited them, Saib would be in the general area. He was to welcome others upon their arrival.

Again, like the fairy tale her parents had read to her from the solitary book she owned as a child, Quiatua felt transported into one. She had tried to pump Saib full of questions; however, he answered few to her satisfaction. Finally, with a whimsical smile toward Quiatua, Saib explained, like she, he was part of the transition as a journey as well. He held limited information and apologized for not having all the answers. Quiatua then found herself climbing over the backboard of the seat and landed in the comfort of the hay again. Time enough, she thought to herself—time enough.

The next day, the cart, horse, Saib, and Quiatua stopped before the village's entrance. She had questioned Saib as to the reason for the stop. Saib had explained they were to see the impressive plan before their entrance. Quiatua peered harder into the short distance and became inspired. She would arrive briefly and become part of the hustle and bustle she had seen. Saib had pointed to a group of people who worked to erect stable structures, and each was to hold people as they began to influx to the area.

Quiatua stated she saw the abundance of trees and wondered why others had yet to build housing in the trees. Saib told her that was only one of her specialties, and then he made a clicking sound, and the horse moved forward. With more wonder, Quiatua stated what an impressive sight, so many fellow people worked in harmony. How on Earth was she to communicate with all these people? Saib gleamed with pleasure and said "Telepathically, of course." She could do the same with him as she had done in the past with Azna. Quiatua had forgotten. She always used her voice with Azna, who answered her telepathically.

Upon arrival at Mabo and Tiao's dwelling, the cart stopped. Quiatua heard an excited shrill from inside, and Tiao exited with Mabo. Telepathically they spoke with Saib and Quiatua, and it took a few moments for Quiatua to catch up with the vibration. What she took from the interaction was Tiao was well pleased they made the journey safely, and she had prepared a part of their home specifically for her. Quiatua felt so loved and special that she could not withhold her pleasure. She reached for Tiao and Mabo as she received the best hug she had missed for so many years. Saib and Mabo gathered Quiatua's bags as the women entered the dwelling. There Quiatua spotted the specific hammock made with such care and decoration just for bear; she felt welcomed like no other time in her life.

2

Quiatua had the next several days to acclimate to the village, the people, the lifestyle, and the wonderful couple that took her into their dwelling. As she worked in unison with others, she became more confident in her abilities as her knowledge of the tree-dwelling structures was immense. With all the referral to the meticulous notes Azna appointed her to write down, she understood the velocity. She continued praising Azna and allowed other Spirit Guides to direct her throughout the days.

While everyone chipped in as needed, Eusia, Rundda, and Warec arrived next. An array of questions entered their thoughts when they were introduced to Mabo. Warec, unfamiliar with telepathic communication, found the most difficulty with his surroundings. He had extensively questioned both Eusia and Rundda before boarding the plane. While on the aircraft, Eusia rested, and Rundda continued to answer as much as possible. Rundda praised Yellow, Warec's Ascended Master, for his strength and consistency in working with Warec. Yellow projected thoughts to Rundda; the appreciation of his efforts was not unnoticed. Tiao and fellow village people had prepared the rooms in their outbuilding around the property. So wonderfully comfortable, Rundda was tempted to nap for a while. Instead, too excited about aiding where needed, he prodded Warec to settle into his room. Surprised by the care offering the room with adjacent bathroom facilities, Warec was pleased with the efforts. Walls adorned with tapestry, woven articles, and blankets; he was stunned by how at home he felt. Warec had a lot of questions answered by Rundda, and he appreciated the thoughts shared. He allowed Rundda to recover from all the questions and followed the villager toward the commotion of working people.

Eusia was given the same intricate emblem worn by Mabo from Tiao, who felt honored to pin it on Eusia. The women shared the same interest in benefiting all who came for healing. Under construction was a dome structure that housed several rooms inside, with the center chosen for Eusia to instruct others in healing energies. Tiao had arranged an assortment of materials, herbs, clean water, crystals, anything she thought Eusia would ask. Eusia was overwhelmed as she told Tiao telepathically the care in the comfort, decorations, all the materials assembled, and, oh, yes, the herbs and clean water, the staple of her teachings, was so thoughtful. The women stepped outside the structure, and Tiao then sounded a horn apparatus, and soon others appeared.

A villager led Rundda toward the tree house formations. He was amazed by the intricate thought process for sanitation with water retention and distribution system. He did not ponder the need to meet the lead person over the project as he traveled the area to find them. A person tried introducing him to Quiatua as she instructed the balancing of beams in a triangle design above their heads. Rundda was stunned by her youth, yet maturity as she directed the activities and shared her notes. The young woman was so intense in sharing her thoughts telepathically Rundda did not want to interrupt. Out of the corner of her eye, she saw Rundda, and without further delay, she jumped at the opportunity to introduce herself. She was ecstatic to meet with the chosen few as they arrived.

3

The villagers and guests settled into a routine when dusk covered the land. They gathered in the center space of the village, bringing with them food, water, clean clothing, and any essential one could need. The feast was abundant, and much care was in preparation for all the hard-working people to enjoy. They toasted nightly to another beautiful day of blessings for being able to work together for the greater good. Quiatua had squealed with delight when she saw Saib appear with the same horse and cart when they entered the area. It had been days since she had seen Saib. So much to relate to him. However, when she approached the cart, she realized he had shuttled in two more of the chosen few.

The horse and cart came to a stop, and Saib introduced Quiatua to Augustin and a very passive Aunewu. The journey by sea and land had been long and taxed the boy. When Augustin tried to move his son, Aunewu jumped at the chance to leave the cart. Then, fully awake, and aware, Aunewu thanked Saib, patted the horse he had named Majestic, slapped his hand in Quiatua's, and grabbed his father's hand with the other. Within a split second, the three were walking toward the center of the village. Aunewu's eyes were again full of wild wonder while Quiatua attempted to communicate telepathically to them.

Frustration mounted quickly for Quiatua, then Azna appeared in her form and corrected the young woman's attitude, for Azna had to communicate with the boy and father first. Finally, Quiatua excused herself and turned toward the center. Azna welcomed both father and son to the village and chose they were to meet with Mabo, who had walked toward them. Mabo considered the language barrier, and Azna suggested that Augustin and Aunewu attempt slow interaction to telepathic communications. After a short introduction, Mabo led the two toward his dwelling first, as they needed to feel welcomed and know where they would stay.

Augustin and Aunewu felt the accommodations to be more than expected and quite pleased. Mabo recognized the look on their faces as such and pointed at a door toward their bathroom facilities. Aunewu was delighted as his bathroom at home was outside of their dwelling, making this quite dangerous overnight due to wild animals. Aunewu attempted his telepathic communications with Mabo, although scrabbled, Mabo smiled broadly at the boy and gestured, 'Well done.' The three of them exited the area and walked toward the center.

Tiao was the first to greet them and communicated she was pleased that Aunewu was included in the transition. Aunewu greeted her with a huge smile and admiration for her and her fellow people of the comfortable accommodations. Aunewu once again tried to communicate this to her. He communicated telepathically with some effort, while Mabo and Tiao had patience. Finally, the hurdle cleared, and he tried to tell the same to his father, who appeared lost in thought. The trio knew Augustine's telepathic communications would come eventually.

Once again, Quiatua joined them and initiated gestures of welcome and understood the journey was long. Augustin and Aunewu welcomed the food, drink, and hospitality of the people. Aunewu initiated communication with Quiatua, Mabo, and Tiao about others and their arrival. The broad smiles told all for information. Aunewu once again grasped his hand in Quiatua's and the other in his father's hand, and the three went ahead toward Eusia, Rundda, and Warec. Mabo and Tiao hugged and offered admiration to the Great Source for bringing all the people together to witness this reset of the World.

4

The ones who had arrived became more acclimated to the village, the outstanding people, the lifestyle, the belief system, and the animals which roamed freely. They marveled at undomestic animals and their calm, quiet, and surrendered mindset. All seemed natural, and they took in the beauty of the life in the area. In addition, they all practiced telepathic communications while becoming accustomed to the other's abilities, skills, and knowledge.

Over the horizon, Saib, the horse, and the cart appeared. Another individual or more was en route to arrive. As the cart drew near the village, the people began a chant, signaling another or more people would come. Mabo and Tiao appeared from nearby the water well with Rundda and walked to meet the cart. Saib designated one more individual to arrive. The horse and cart stopped, and Samuel appeared from the hay at the rear. Anxious to stretch his muscles, he jumped from the cart enthusiastically. His eyes were filled with wild wonder as three people extended genuine smiles toward him. Bewildered, Samuel looked for Saib to break the silence between all.

Saib telepathically introduced the three to Samuel. The lack of communication mystified Samuel, or so he thought. Then, Luna, his Ascended Master, acknowledged his lack of understanding. She signaled for Samuel to begin as they had practiced, communicating telepathically. Oh yes, the telepathic communication thing. Difficult as it seemed for Samuel, he had practiced with Luna, Saib, and even Majestic, the horse. As the horse had explained to Samuel, he was a no-named horse until the kind boy, Aunewu, named him. Samuel was startled when he could telecommunicate with the horse. All the years of study and while he worked with animals, he could have harnessed his mental capability and telecommunicated with them!

Since he had the vision and heard the words, the bizarre days seemed to collimate into these moments. Samuel was grateful to see generous, smiling people, yet he longed to see the familiar faces of Katerina and Suri. Tiao gestured for Samuel to open his mind, and when he did, he saw the two women as they embarked on the final part of their journey. Samuel felt like his waist and knees were to give out on him as Mabo and Rundda reached to steady him. Yet, upon their touch, Samuel felt immense peace and stability in the events as they unfolded. He glanced around the beautiful setting, where the air seemed so clean, as the plants and trees thrived in the environment.

From the corner of his eye, Samuel caught a glimpse of a large type of bird, and he swore it stared at him. Rundda laughed, and Mabo explained that the bird protected the village. Rundda apologized for the laughter and said he thought the same upon his first encounter with Onyx, the bird protector. Onyx indeed checked out all those who entered the village; if not of positive energy, the giant bird would carry the encountered away. Samuel telepathically communicated with the three individuals, "Good to know and remember." Luna expressed her pleasure with Samuel and his successful attempt at telepathic communication. She told them to introduce themselves further, then faded into a mist.

Rundda returned to the task at the water well while Mabo and Tiao traveled toward Samuel's sleeping quarters. Before the entrance of the building, a large feline animal appeared, stretched out their extended body, and crawled into a ball as a sound emanated from deep inside the animal. Samuel found himself alarmed and bewildered by the animal, the sound, and the proximity to the three of them. Mabo jumped at the opportunity to communicate with Samuel telepathically and said no fear, as all animals you will meet here are not inclined to devour you. Samuel, mystified, stammered in his thoughts and questioned both; how was this possible? All wild animals will devour you and must be kept at a distance after all! Tiao then stated as complex as the concept seemed, it was not so. Animals and humans were meant to roam the Earth freely and live harmoniously. Instead, man became the hunter and destroyed the harmony, not the animals.

Tiao explained to Samuel that the animals he would encounter were not domesticated and considered sacred to their relationship with them. After all his years of study and animal interaction, the thoughts were beyond Samuel's comprehension. He always wanted closer contact with animals at the zoo besides having to sedate them or stay a safe distance nearby the habitats and forewarned those who did not respect the animals' space. Mabo and Tiao smiled their generous smiles as Mabo told Samuel that he was in for a lifetime journey. He and Tiao excused themselves to allow Samuel to settle into his quarters and take in the magnificent feline animal near the entrance.

5

Samuel found his place among all those who had arrived. He admired Eusia, who practiced holistic healing from Reiki to crystals to sound and herbal attributes as he learned and offered his knowledge in unison. Warec and for his sideways look at all those who presented new ideas to him and considered them. Rundda, as he proved his knowledge of water and sewage distribution, which helped the village and the Earth. Quiatua for her unencumbered views of the World, how she truly lived off the land and taught others, and received information as she added to her notebook. The magnificent loyalty from the villagers toward their beloved Mabo and Tiao, who they so cherished for the inspiration from the Great Source. Aunewu's relentless energy and inquiries of efforts toward the transition. His father's concern that the boy should halter some of his enthusiasm. The large feline never left their presence, and the group named him Zeus as they felt him to be from the Source as one of the many protectors sent.

Communication was sent toward the group, and Samuel spun around when he received the love which emanated from the energy. He knew he had felt this sensation prior, and sure enough, Suri and Katerina had arrived. With great anticipation, Samuel projected his thoughts toward the others as he introduced the women to the group. His excitement was so intense that his ideas were scrambled. All in the group recognized his appreciation for the women who had walked closer. The genuine smiles on the women's faces were undeniable; they had such peace.

Suri telepathically communicated with all. She and Katerina were pleased to make the journey safely. She added the fact that Katerina was the person who had received the vision and words, that she was honored and grateful for being in everyone's presence. The group received the information and welcomed both women. Katerina and Suri were so excited with the prospect and progress of the massive educational structure; they at once began to aid. Katerina explained to the others where the women were when she had received the vision and words, as all worked on the progress together.

Katerina explained she was a Geophysicist with studies in other fields, while Suri was a superior Mathematician. The words of admiration from Katerina toward Suri were not unnoticed, and the others felt the energy of love the women shared. Both women's Ascended Masters had prepared them with the practice of telepathic communications and the visions of the others with their talents, knowledge, and abilities. The women were excited to meet the people of the group and could not wait to learn from their abilities.

Energy emanated from Quiatua regarding her insecurities about inadequate talents, knowledge, and life skills. Suri felt the power and sent her loving thoughts, and she nodded her head to Katerina; the young woman would need their aid. Knowing well, they had much to gain from Quiatua's resilience, sense of freedom, and ability to live off the land. The group sent loving energy to Quiatua, acknowledged her insecurities, and verified that she was not alone, as all did not know what was to come next. Eusia sent energy that the time had arrived for group meditation. Without delay, everyone but Warec welcomed the thought. Rundda projected the visualization of Warec out on a log alone, with no paddle or direction, just floating with the water current. The others smiled at one another, and Warec, stunned, vibrated the energy that was precisely how he had felt the past weeks.

Without further delay, Mabo motioned with his arm toward Warec to move forward to the meditation. Mabo knew through his Ascended Master, Formli, Warec had lacked a significant part of his life from spiritual belief and support. Tiao sent loving thoughts to all in the area, which clarified the moment for all: we are all in this together, now get in here! A little chant was audible as the villagers agreed, and the group came together for the meditation and toward the next part of the journey.

CHAPTER 6

The Ascended Masters assembled occasionally to revisit the prospect and progress humans had made. Some Masters had projected their concerns, while others trusted the process. Love and light vibrations were cast toward the Earth, which resonated with the life forms—time was drawing near—time of the reset— time of a great transition. The animals, plant life, soil, air quality, and water of the oceans, seas, rivers, and creeks echoed sighs of relief. The chosen Ascended Masters continued their updates with Omarya, Akaham, and Maik.

Interaction toward the World from the Great Source was also in progress— harmful toxins and waste were collected and then expelled toward the most bottomless black hole in the universe. Diabolical thoughts and oppression from humanity began to lift. For those who held these actions, they fell to sleep and did not awaken. Areas of the World became free from the oppressors while some humans tried to continue the activity. As these humans continued their desire to oppress, they also fell asleep during their immediate action and did not awaken. Upon occasional interaction with Akaham and Maik, the Masters learned that those oppressive souls were escorted and dissolved into the same black hole. Cruel and unusual punishment toward animals and plant life ended. These humans' souls were escorted and dissolved in the black hole.

Political environments around the World took notice of the change. Freed human voices rang out of distrust toward government institutions that had not appealed to the masses. No repercussions were to come to these humans with an unwritten rule: To let no person interfere with the freedom of the people to use their voices. The voices were rising in solidarity throughout the World, which meant repressive action was transformed. No longer would harm, imprisonment, mutilation, or death come to those who used their voices. Humans of the Earth began to feel the comfort of freedom, leading most toward a universal belief system.

The Great Source sent love and light toward humans with mental, physical, and emotional ailments. These humans slowly felt relief from the constrictions caused by these ailments. However, some suffered from life-long restrictions, and others experienced long-term and short-term effects. The humans who experienced this slow lift from their limitations benefited from the introduction to their Spirit Guides. These Guides instructed the humans with immediate caregivers, facilities, physicians, and necessary apparatus or aides.

The Ascended Masters generated thoughts toward misusing narcotics, alcohol, prescription drugs, tobacco, and by-products. They gave instructions to these humans for redemption from their discretions, and the Guides were to aid these humans. The process was a slow withdrawal with aid from the holistic healers with herbal medicinal, sound healing, Reiki, and crystal healing aid. Most humans affected would require stays in facilities to make the transition complete. The World Health Organization would administer the care and expense with collaboration from public and private facilities. The Masters monitored the aftercare of the humans. Some felt extreme difficulties and were placed in a cocooned suspension state. This state would allow for a reset of the human's mindset, spiritual and physical bodies to heal for eternity.

Most Guides and Masters generated thought toward the famine of human beings in different areas of the World. At the same time, staples would be released from the oppressors. They allowed the freedom to have the food items shipped to all areas. With the lifted restrictions, the World's state of malnutrition would dissipate. The Guides were to aid in distributing the staples with excessive needs being done so with fairness to all humans. Cleaner water would be given from the Earth as pollutants dissipated, allowing the water to flow freely toward the surface. The Worlds Kitchen Organization would administer the care and expense of staples with collaboration from public and private generous donations as gratefulness and nonmaterialistic mindsets evolved.

Great concern was generated toward the incarcerated humans due to their actions, war, or political imprisonment, and instructions were given for the Guides to screen the humans of the war and political imprisonment first. Then, the Guides were to present those humans falsely accused or involuntarily placed as war criminals to the Master Council. The undertaking would require thoroughness and patience as many humans were in the status. Upon these humans being reconciled and released, the Guides were to help with their human life transition. The Master Council would oversee the incarcerated humans on a one-by-one basis. Many Masters began the task immediately, as several knew of humans who had redeemed themselves and needed the favor of the Source to be released and become productive members of society. For those humans who were dark-natured or had malicious thought processes, they would remain incarcerated until further instructions.

Many considerations and instructions occurred as the Guides and Masters worked in harmony—the transition emerged in animal life, water, atmosphere, and soil. This energy was projected toward the Earth while the chosen humans worked to usher in the next lifestyle of humankind.

CHAPTER 7

Aunewu found telepathic communication easier while his father, Augustin, struggled with the process. Aunewu updated his mother daily through contact with his Ascended Master, Dyne. His mother, Haou, was pleased with the contact and knew her spouse would also develop the ability. She was ecstatic because the group was so considerate to her son and spouse; they allowed patience with Aunewu. Haou knew her son could be curious about all aspects of life, animals, plant life, water source, and the air they breathed. Dyne communicated with the visualizations as Aunewu, Katerina, and Suri discovered the universe, atmosphere, scientific and mathematical reasoning, and equations. The group and Aunewu took in as much information as a time would come when they returned to their own continents again.

The group found Aunewu's compassion and kindness extraordinary for the boy's age and gradually understood why he was chosen. Aunewu was granted walks alongside the large feline Zeus, where he found various kinds of animals, insects, and fowl needing care. He brought them directly to Samuel and Eusia, where he would learn their condition. The healing process would begin with the aid of Samuel and Eusia, while Warec consulted for the pharmaceuticals needs of the species, then shifted to herbal equivalents. These newfound learnings benefited humans in the immediate area, and most knew of the benefits while others adopted the practice. Finally, the treasure trove of nature's gift for all on Earth was allowed.

Aunewu's intuitions and inquiries were taken seriously, spawning others to question. For instance, would all wild and untrusted animals become docile like those nearby the village? As Samuel was a zoologist, this was of utmost importance to him. He understood that humanity could live in harmony with any species. Samuel had seen the detrimental effects of humans on animals while on Earth. He hoped that all species would not feel threatened or fear being hunted and knew firsthand how helpful this could be for them. Samuel's thought process and hopes stayed within the group and villagers. Quiatua projected a visualization of time at her dwelling with all animals in the area. Large and small, considered dangerous, all seemed docile within her presence. As she explained, the species were docile toward her because she knew no other way but to give them respect and space.

Quiatua cheered Aunewu on with his ability to consider the same for all species he crossed in the nearby area. Aunewu was overjoyed and explained that Zeus contributed to the effects on the nearby species. Zeus gave out energy to all species, which commanded humans and animals to dwell on the Earth as one. No longer would harm, negligence, abuse, death, or the hunt of any animal species be needed. Animals from the area sighed in unison and regarded the message sent through Zeus to be from the Great Source. Quiatua would be seen in stillness, meditation, and prayer when animal species approached her without harm. The awesomeness of the sight spurred all others in the area to generate the same energy and light for the inhabitants.

The group and villagers appreciated Quiatua's knowledge of tree dwellings. With further understanding, they realized the places were safer from floods. The sense of peace living among the limbs, leaves, and animals would be a constant reminder of humans and animals living in harmony. The dwelling's water retention and waste distribution had come far. With Rundda's knowledge added, numerous residences were underway. Quiatua remembered her knowledge of clay and hay- based structures from her parent's dwelling. Facilities in the area made from those materials, would alleviate the need to cut the wood for future reference.

All agreed to begin eliminating cut lumber and acclimate to the clay and hay for ground dwellings.

The villagers shared their knowledge of plant life and the growing of edible vegetation for the community. Quiatua, Eusia, Augustin, and Rundda achieved great success with their expertise while adding their skills to the task. Different regions of the World had their varieties, and all in the group wondered what types could acclimate to their areas. Samuel, Tiao, Mabo, and Quiatua knew the herbs used for various ailments and the production of human balance. They learned much from the villagers and contributed their knowledge to excel in the process with the native plant life. All continued to learn and contribute to the experience of growing the mass vegetation and herbals needed for the transition.

Warec stood amazed by the work completed in tandem between everyone and took in all the knowledge with vigor. He contributed to the questions, research, and progress of converting pharmaceutical needs to herbal and plant remedies. When he questioned the human lives which needed support by medications or procedures, such as dialysis, Yallow, his Ascended Master, would answer. Most humans with advanced illnesses would have them alleviated from the state at that time and need vegetable and herbal remedies. Warec felt the daunting task lifted from his responsibilities and began to excel in the process—written notes on materials supplied by Mabo and Tiao were secured appropriately in binders. The information flowed so quickly for Warec; he was astounded by the process and enthralled by the vision these materials would appear in all regions of the World during the transition. He no longer felt his work was underappreciated.

The villagers and group appreciated Warec's knowledge and efforts. They saw firsthand his apprehension of the process, which, when he dismissed, resurrected him toward his highest work. Warec started to feel he could not conduct his most significant efforts without the Ascended Masters. The Ascended Masters had sent Warec numerous Ascended Healers to answer questions, aid in research, and fill him with peace toward the process. Eusia was invigorated by the help and found the interaction for other skeptics Worldwide to experience the same support. She was pleased as she knew the witness of the integration was changing more thought processes. While she and Warec, with the others, worked in tandem, she glanced from time to time to all and smiled. The age of inner healing, peace, and work to be completed rose.

Eusia yearned for a deeper divine interaction for the healings she gave through Reiki, sound, crystal, and herbal remedies. The group and villagers excelled in their thought process to aid humans in the healings she and Rundda demonstrated and performed. She acquired information through the Ascended Healers and Masters, who were pleased with Eusia's ability to explain learned processes. Eusia's grand elders were the foundation for her ability to heal; she thanked them daily. Now she felt closer to those present on Earth and those great spirits who had passed on the knowledge. If ever she felt blocked, she called on Peluan, her Ascended Master. Together they worked through the block and gained further help from the Ascended Healers. She foresaw how healing would occur after the transition.

Peluan and the Healers explained that all would be well with Eusia and the group. The humans around the World who healed would receive a message of contact with the Ascended Healers. All questions, answers, research, consultations, and verbal and visual communication would come through a handheld device unfamiliar with that part of South America. Some humans would reach Eusia to aid in the healing through the Worldwide internet. The Healers explained this technology was used Worldwide, and devices would be delivered once all negativity was dispelled. The device, connection, and delivery would be free of charge to the citizens of the World. However, this internet was used for the good of the World. Any humans who tried to form negativity on the internet would be an instant notification for the Great Source to intervene. With a sigh of relief from Eusia, she was reassured the Great Source was good!

Katerina and Suri found themselves in a loop, drifting from the group, to villagers and toward the outskirts of the village with Zeus. The isolation they felt in Antarctica had disappeared with the journey. For almost a year, they had stayed in a doomed dwelling with others nearby in a steel-enforced structure. Most were scientists, mathematicians, a cook, and other career-minded people. Katerina and Suri felt welcomed by the group; for the first time in a long time, they did not feel isolated as a couple. They chimed in and worked together well with all. The women worked artistically with Warec, as he was confident and a perfectionist, and with

Samuel, they all laughed and enjoyed their bond. They had learned a great deal in a short amount of time from both men.

Aunewu ran the group with his inquisitive mind and in search of all things new to him and his father. While Augustin tried to keep up with Aunewu, the women helped him. They accommodated Aunewu's interest in Mathematics, Physics, Geometry, and other subjects for his experience. He certainly was a brilliant boy, and they communicated telepathically with his mother Haou, and gave her scenarios and visions of his antics. Augustin had expressed, on occasions to all, his appreciation. He knew Aunewu liked Suri, and the boy felt closest to her because her hugs felt like his mother's, which he missed.

Here the women found peace with the group and village. To them, it was unfathomable how the villagers had stretched out their arms, homes, and lifestyle with the group. All visitors were welcomed as if no one was a stranger, as if they knew they would usher in a new way of life on Earth for some time. Both women admired Eusia, Rundda, Quiatua, Mabo, and Tiao. These people seemed so grounded, apt at their skills and abilities, and most of all, so spiritual. Late into the night, the women consulted with Mabo and Tiao, and they learned so much of the spiritual World, which they needed. Mabo and Tiao always seemed to enjoy these late-night talks. For them, the blessing had arrived. More and more people would experience love and light, and Mabo and Tiao felt this was their lives mission.

Suri had pain in her left side for some time, and she felt the time had come for help. Without further delay, Mabo introduced the gift of healing to Suri through Eusia and Rundda. Once consulted, immediate sessions began with the aid of the Ascended Healers and Spirit Guides. Suri had a blockage in her intestines which surprised and scared both women. However, the blockage became a non-issue quickly because of the guidance of meditation, visualization, sound therapy, and Reiki. Suri was astounded by the process; she fell on her knees in the middle of the village and cried out to the Great Source: "For You are so good." As the villagers agreed, and soon a chant began.

The chants always resonated with gratitude and were contagious even for 'the visitors' as named by the villagers. With smiles, outstretched arms, and movements of bodies as they swayed into dances, an outpouring of glee was felt. All in the group took part, although apprehensively at first, then all self- consciousness was gone, and freedom of movement roared. The group felt buoyant with the Great Source while Mabo, Tiao, and the villagers expressed their pleasure with the expansion for the others. Joyous freedom in spirit and living should have always been the way of the World; why was it not this way—they wondered? Ascended Healers contributed to the group and villagers, which stretched their experience and catapulted their knowledge. All were eager to achieve their highest and gain help. They welcomed the highest energy from the Great Source and Ascended Masters. The work was relentless, yet none of the group or villagers felt fatigued.

CHAPTER 8

An assembly was held as the group's progress was seen by Omarya. The Masters felt honored when Akaham and Maik appeared, as these energies were direct from the Great Source. However, Akaham and Maik brought forth a visualization and words from the Great Source. The Ascended Masters quieted their thought processes and allowed space for visualization. A cloud appeared, and the Masters learned of diabolical thought processes from some humans to end the transition of Earth.

Upon conclusion of the vision and words, the Ascended Masters were not astonished. When each Master had a lifetime on Earth, some humans tried to control regions, countries, cities, humans, animals, and plant life. The thought process of some human dictators had not changed. On the contrary, as predicted through the Great Source, it had worsened. What was of overall interest to these people was the depletion of the human spirit, and it generated attempts with the thought process and physical action. The reaction to the humans' action was swift, as previously appointed by the Great Source.

What the humans believed were covert operations, signals, sketches, and careful attention to developments of encrypted words, did not go unnoticed. Great Source allowed time to pass for all humans recruited to be revealed. Ascended Masters, Maik, Akaham, and Omarya, with an army of the Blessed Ones—called Angels by most humans, kept a constant overlook of the humans' actions and reported directly to the Great Source. Some human dictators attempted to launch missiles toward other parts of Earth, but not one rocket was launched. None decimated the local area or region where deployment was attempted.

Nothing was released from humans who tried to free hazardous materials into the airstream or biochemical sabotage on the Earth. Instead, the humans who attempted were placed into a whirlwind and escorted to a designated black hole. The same actions were taken upon the humans who tried to decimate the Earth with missiles. No human thoughts of negativity toward the Earth and its inhabitants went unnoticed. The numbers of humans with these thoughts had increased, and Great Source attended at once to the humans—redemption only for those humans who others had naively misled. The spirits were cocooned for these individuals to reinforce the next task at hand for the Earth—peace, oneness, healing, and cooperation among its inhabitants.

Ascended Masters and some Spirit Guides in attendance were given instructions and aid to honor the transition of Earth. Without further delay, tasks were increased, and the Masters paired themselves with the Guides. More Blessed Ones were considered necessary from Great Source as Akaham and Maik designated the groups of Masters and Guides that would assist. With numbers increasing for organization and aid, a cloud formed.

The energy increased significantly, and all in attendance bowed their power in honor. Great Source summoned the area to clear any thought process. The visualization appeared with a group of humans at a water's edge of a large river with a volatile current. Large trucks with corrosive material symbols were present on the bank. A huge concern of thought process filled the assembly. Omarya raised his energy to still the commotion and pointed attention to the cloud. The group of humans were visible in a hurried pace in the attempt to empty the trucks into the river. Large hoses connected to the trucks, and operators scrambled to press levers and knobs to release the contents. The assembled projected thoughts to urge the Great Source to aid in ending the attempt.

No substance was dispelled into the river when the knobs and levers were operated. With a crack of lightning and the audible sound of thunder, individuals involved were struck with a sleep state of their brains and physical bodies. No redemption was called for these humans, as their intentions were well-known before the action. Great Source allowed the demonstration to emphasize the scope of some humans and their attempts to end the transition of Earth. The discernment of the Great Source was resonated and felt by all in the assembly without disbelief, as told by Akaham and Maik, those humans who attempted to harm or end the transition of Earth had no cause to continue their lifetimes. These actions would be terminated, and those spirits would be escorted to the black hole.

The cloud dissipated as Maik continued her thought process. She resonated with the thought that not all humans would have no redemption; those subjected to involuntary diabolic actions had their spirits cocooned to readjust the energies. Maik then projected to the assembled that these attempts were widespread Worldwide and careful consideration was given before the activities, as seen in the example. Akaham interjected: let no mistake be made that Great Source was well informed and aware of these humans and their attempts to end the transition of Earth. With disappointment, Great Source had no further reaction for these humans but to escort the spirits to the black hole, as no redemption would ever be large enough.

The assembly concluded with the emphasis that no Ascended Master, Blessed One, or Spirit Guide would be able to alter the actions of the Great Source. As Akaham projected, Earth's transition had begun; those humans who tried to harm would perish. Great Source had allowed an Earth reset before in several attempts to right the wrong of diabolic humans, which meant the time had arrived; these humans had completed their spiritual walk on Earth.

CHAPTER 9

Quiatua was elated when she grabbed her belongings and shot past the door opening of her accommodations so carefully designed by Tiao. She had felt the urge to speak with Mabo and Tiao about inhabiting one of the tree dwellings the evening before. With glee in their eyes, they had predicted the move, for they both saw in Quiatua a free spirit, one that was unencumbered by traditional dwellings. The couple reflected momentarily on how quickly advanced the group had become and had seen Quiatua's excitement about bringing the option to the area.

In her cooperation with everyone in the area, Quiatua instructed others with enthusiasm and patience. She offered her notes, sketches, and mathematical equations for the dwellings. To her, it was unimaginable why all humans did not dwell among the trees. Others saw her Spirit Guide, Azna, appear and added mindfulness in quest for all the comforts Quiatua had prior. Some villagers and group members communicated telepathically with Azna and were never pushed away from her undivided attention. Azna was grateful to everyone in the area who had welcomed Quiatua's infectious laughter, love, and light. She knew Quiatua had found a place, her people, her tribe, and this brought joy to her.

Samuel was on the outskirts of the village with Zeus and Onyx when he saw Quiatua as she ran toward her chosen tree dwelling. However, Samuel thought she was to leave the area and was in quite a hurry. He glanced around to place where Saib, Majestic, and the cart was for Quiatua's travels. He wondered what may have happened when he discovered they were not in sight. Zeus and Onyx retreated to the nearby forest area while Samuel traveled toward where Quiatua had arrived. With glee in her eye, she saw Samuel's approach, and a huge smile spread across her face. Quiatua announced she would dwell among the trees, the branches, the leaves, and in the air.

Samuel knew her lifestyle and was eager to help bring up her belongings. Without a lift yet built, Quiatua had welcomed the offer of help. Samuel inquired about some rope to swing over the branches to aid as a lift. Unfortunately, nothing of the sort was seen in the immediate area, and without further thought, Quiatua gathered vines from the ground or the readily available trees. As they both worked together, they spoke of the adventure. How was the feeling so different than that of living on the ground? What did the gravitational pull feel like when so high and suspended off the ground? Most of all, did one want to be so far off the ground when using the bathroom?

Quiatua laughed with amusement at all of Samuel's inquiries. For she knew this would be better for him to experience himself. With the last vines placed accordingly, she and Samuel put her belongings in an oval-shaped basket. While the long-tied vines end to end were thrown up to a branch. She designated to Samuel, good to go! And without even one stair put into place yet, she began to climb the tree. Samuel stood poised to catch her; well, just in case, he had thought to himself. She was perched on an upper deck within a short time, squarely looking down at him. She motioned for him to make his way up the tree as she retrieved the basket.

With hesitation, Samuel tried to duplicate the steps she had made when she climbed the tree. He felt lightheaded and needed to end the attempt. However, Quiatua swung the vine-made rope toward him and gestured to him to strap it around his waist. He braced himself against a colossal limb and positioned the vine rope. With a thumbs-up motion toward Quiatua, she braced herself for his weight against the rope. With the reassurance of the activity at hand, he began to climb. Again, with a glee in her eye, she waited for him to make the last part of the ascension. Upon reaching the upper deck, Samuel saw a hand come forward and gladly accepted the help. With some maneuvering, Samuel sat on the edge of the upper deck, inhaled deeply, and pushed his body weight further back.

Quiatua was perched at the edge with bent knees as her legs dangled. Samuel felt his stomach lunge downward, and Quiatua understood. Tree dwelling was not for the light of heart or for those who had a fear of falling. She allowed some moments to pass; in the stillness, she closed her eyes, raised her arms toward the sky, and offered thanks for her newfound comfort. Oh, how she had wanted this place since her arrival. Samuel sat quietly for a moment, then when he had caught his breath, he opened his eyes and realized the wonder around him. A slow smile crept across his face, and Quiatua noticed. She allowed him time to acclimate, quiet himself, and reflect on the beauty.

Ah, yes, another human who could appreciate the abundance of all that surrounded them. Samuel was unsure of the experience but thoroughly enjoyed the view and peace within his being. His consciousness connected to his body as he pulled his knees toward his chest and wrapped them with his arms. He wanted to rock back and forth on his buttocks for some reason, but for fear of looking ridiculous, he did not. Quiatua had learned a great deal from the villagers about body language, and as if she read his mind, she pulled her waist backward with her arms, pulled her knees toward her chest, and wrapped them with her arms. She then began to rock on her buttocks. Samuel appreciated the gesture and laughed. This extraordinary, free-spirited young woman was fun!

The two talked to one another like they were long-lost family members, like siblings. Rocked and talked, caught up with one another about their experiences since their arrival, the knowledge they had gained, their love for the Earth, the animal kingdom and kindness, plant life, the atmosphere, no worries of war, famine, or disease, or as Quiatua had stated; dis-ease. Quiatua admitted she was seeing and learning extensively from Samuel and Warec and was grateful for the knowledge. Samuel felt a flush cross his face, but most of all, he felt honored. Honored he could spread his love of the animal kingdom and herbal knowledge. At the same time, he admitted to her his admiration of how she could quiet herself and go into a peaceful state, her zone, how the animals came to her without hesitation and nestled next to or nearby her.

Quiatua gave Samuel an all-knowing smile across her face, nodded her head, stood up, and invited him to explore the inside of the dwelling. He stood upright, gained his bearings, refused to glance over the edge, and acknowledged his need to build the railings. Samuel had been so involved and in-depth with research Warec, Eusia, Rundda, Mabo, Tiao, and he had undertaken he was less engaged with the tree dwellings. Nevertheless, he discovered a high, slanted ceiling with exposed timber bracings, a sturdy woven thatched bed, a small rectangular timber table with two thatched chairs, a two-person couch, and a sink—what a sink! Quiatua laughed again with amusement and explained all the comforts of a home in the trees. After all, Rundda's specialty was water catchment and distribution, let alone waste distribution.

Wait a moment, waste distribution? Indeed, Quiatua had nodded her head toward a timber-built door. Lo and behold, to Samuel's amazement, there was a wet room bath area behind the door. How could this be as such? Quiatua explained although the materials were different in the local area, Rundda and she had devised somewhat of the same. A catchment system above the room or to the side gravity- fed the water downward, and viola, you have running water through cane used as pipes. Pull up on a manufactured lever to flow water or push down the lever to stop the flow. Brilliant, Samuel thought out loud, ingenious! Better yet, check out the toilet and waste distribution system, Quiatua gestured. Sure enough, under a manufactured toilet lid was a seat, a box, and what was this item, a lever again. Press down on the lever with your foot Quiatua gestured. Astonishingly the water flowed from the box inside and disappeared out the bottom of the floor.

In disbelief, Samuel walked outside toward the platform, laid on his stomach, braced his hands on a sturdy branch, and lowered his head. What he did not see on his climb up the tree was the ingenuity of two connected minds. Rundda and Quiatua had joined cane pipes and vines under the platform, down the tree toward the ground, and at a 45-degree angle, had the line meet with cane pipe on the ground. Samuel could view from that height the complex cane pipes laid out below as a tube maze toward the edge of the village beyond an uninhabited area into the forest. The realization of the feat came to Samuel's mind as he moved his body backward, gained his bearings, and slowly stood.

He marveled at the engineering, the precise layout needed, and the need to connect all other tree dwellings similarly. He glanced at Quiatua, who waited for his reaction. Then it came; a vast smile reached across his face, and this brought joy to Quiatua. Like Samuel had his ability, as did all the group and villagers, she also had hers. This ability would go far beyond the area's borders, out to the World that desperately needed the infrastructure. Samuel stood and shook his head in amazement at the accomplishment, and he knew then the two of them needed to connect on more knowledge. Quite pleased with herself, Quiatua had gathered some of her belongings and headed inside to place them. Samuel had been happy to oblige with help, and he smiled broadly when his hands crossed the top of the bear's head, carefully placed inside Tiao's handmade hammock.

2

The conversation was disrupted when both heard Rundda's voice call to them. With urgency, all were to meet at the newly constructed educational dome, as Rundda announced. Without delay, Samuel motioned for Quiatua to aid in his descent down the tree. Once complete, Quiatua swung down on the vine to the ground while both men shook their heads in astonishment. Then, relieved, she was safe; Quiatua outstretched her arms, bent her elbows, stood before both men, and gestured for them to join her. Both men walked toward her, one on each side, bent their elbows, and the trio walked arm and arm toward the dome quickly.

The villagers and others of the group had arrived and knelt in anticipation. Once the trio settled, the energy in the area shifted. The Ascended Masters of the group began to appear slowly as their power adjusted to the atmospheric conditions. With great appreciation for their presence, the assembled bowed and waited until Mabo communicated telepathically. Next, the introduction of the Ascended Masters and some Spirit Guides were made. Tiao shared next, that she had received the message that the Great Source was to send the Masters present, and she felt honored to have been the chosen one for communications. The Ascended Masters and Guides bowed toward her direction, straightened themselves, and settled their energy.

Yallow, Warec's Ascended Master, projected his thought process first. He gave information to all gathered, the energy of the Earth had shifted dramatically, and the Great Source considered an assembly essential. As Yallow went on, he stated numerous Earth inhabitants were not acclimating to the shift toward the transition well. These humans were instructed through their Spirit Guides to gather some belongings and prepare for travel. A great commotion of words and energy filled the area. With a gesture from Azna, Quiatua's Spirit Guide, the uproar was to be quieted, the power to be stabilized. Many in attendance glanced toward Mabo and Tiao, who had raised their hands downward to aid. Some had a fearful expressions and their eyes darted in anxiety.

With permission from the Masters, Mabo communicated for all to close their eyes, inhale, and exhale slowly. Mabo continued and reminded those present that the moments ahead were those that he had spoken of prior. To realize the Great Source chose the village, villagers and those gathered. With great relief in the area, the energy was changed, and Mabo's smile resonated; all was well. Those present shifted their stance and began to settle for the information that was presented. The Masters and Guides beamed with brilliant light and love as they joined the others in the position.

Eusia's Ascended Master, Peluan, continued the thought process and projected the numerous inhabitants would arrive soon. He cast the admiration the Great Source had for all in attendance. The motivation, progress, collaboration, precise attention to detail and comfort for those about to arrive had not gone unnoticed. All in attendance bowed at their waist and felt honored. Their efforts were so motivated by love for the Earth and the desire to help in all ways they could for the good of humanity. Peluan projected thoughts of Eusia and Rundda's abilities they had gained during interaction with the Ascended Healer, Masters, and Guides. However, they would need further aid from all in attendance.

Those inhabitants who were to arrive, needed in-depth aid in healing. Peluan projected thoughts that other humans in the regional area would travel toward the village. These humans and the villagers would help Eusia, Rundda, Katerina, Suri, Samuel, Mabo, and Tiao through received communications for the healings. Upon their arrival, Warec, Aunewu,

Augustin, and others would fortify these efforts in any possible way. The Great Source would notice the actions and plenty of resources would arrive. Mabo's Ascended Master, Formli, projected thoughts of admiration for all in attendance and visualized how all had gathered with their efforts in unison to that present time. Formli cast thoughts of completing the task and how all present had felt physically exhausted but pleased with their accomplishments. Formli acknowledged, the humans' feelings would materialize from time to time, even when the chosen ones returned to their continents.

Katerina's Ascended Master, Koyro, with permission from the Ascended Masters, continued to project his thoughts to all. He visualized the Earth's transition taking place and humans on Earth who had experienced trauma due to territorial wars. The injustice the humans expressed in anger, the sense of loss, the depression, and the loss of family and friends were heard. These were some of the humans to arrive who needed immediate aid. Great care and admiration would be required. These humans needed a sense of stability, relaxed day-to-day interactions, and more substance of food and clean water than their bodies could manage upon arrival. Koyro projected Great Source had ended the territorial wars, and some humans wanted to end their lives after the termination. These humans had been placed in a sleep state, and their physical bodies were cocooned. This procedure allowed the humans spirit to reconnect with the Great Source. Their bodies and brains were in a recuperation state.

Koyro then gestured toward Suri, Katerina, Tiao, Mabo, and Quiatua. With great energy, he offered a blessing from Great Source. The gift was to pay particular attention to all Eusia, Rundda, and other chosen healers who would arrive and the healing process. These abilities would go with them further than they could imagine in the future. Samuel was appointed as the person who would record the interactions with all involved in the healings. Sporadically he would travel among the elected areas with a furnished recording device. These recordings would be stored and uploaded to the next internet. Samuel's Ascended Master, Luna, gestured toward him and offered an uplifting visualization. Although the task would be daunting; he would have the aid of others. Luna made her point clear that all humans would need to reach this skill level to help in all areas of the World. Luna, along with Spirit Guides, would help Samuel and the others.

Aunewu saw the opportunity to raise his arm for a question. The energy in the space lightened, and Akaham gestured for the boy to stand and communicate. Augustin shifted uncomfortably, not aware of the question or implications. He still was unsettled with the considerable undertaking the whole World was to encounter. Aunewu shot straight up from his position, inhaled deeply, exhaled slowly, and smiled. Akaham gestured, when he was ready, to go ahead. Aunewu told all he could help Samuel intermittently; he wanted to learn this new device called a 'recorder.' The air in the area lightened significantly, and the other children agreed aloud they wished to assist; please, please, please? Without further delay, Akaham manifested a practice recording device, traveled toward Aunewu, and gestured for the other children to come close. Aunewu's smile told every emotion he had in his mind. Other children glanced at their parents or elders for permission. Then, with glee in their bodies, they stood and traveled toward Akaham, their auras filled with light and love as they journeyed. Spirit Guides appeared and gestured applause. They had watched and waited for the moments when more children became a part of the transition in full force.

Akaham bent his energy toward their level, and he projected thoughts that each child could have one device. These devices were for practice, and they would also learn how to use, care for, upload the information, and store the devices. The children of the Earth were the generation that needed as much information from now on; they were the generation that would care for the elders. The children came into Akaham's energy, the first humans to do so. The children felt instant love, admiration, care, and happiness. They became joyous, looked upon Akaham and the device with wonder, and felt a more significant part of the transition. Maik traveled toward the group, and the children knelt and bowed. Maik and Akaham stood in their energy, bent toward the power, blessed each of them, and gestured a hug in the middle of the encompassed area.

All gathered were amazed by the generosity of Maik and Akaham. Up to this point, other than Aunewu, the parents and elders thought it best for the children to be seen and not heard. The children shined like beacons of light; their happiness was pure and content. Maik and Akaham read the energy in the area and sent loving thoughts to all. On the contrary, the children were a gateway to all the Earth to experience, once again, unconditional love. Tears filled the eyes of some gathered, and others reached out for the blessings. Some crumpled into fetal positions. They so wanted the feeling of unconditional love. But, once again, all present felt the sense, and all was good.

With the energies dispelled, some had to recover while Mabo gestured for permission to communicate. Akaham, pleased with the gesture, granted permission. Mabo produced thoughts to all present, and all those who would remain on Earth were truly loved. Excellent care, love, and energy would be poured onto the others who would arrive, not to forget the passion felt at the moment—unconditional love. Akaham and Maik gestured upwards with their thoughts and produced the holiest words toward the Great Source-Amen.

3

With such vigor and sacredness in the area, Akaham and Maik began to dissipate with the Ascended Masters, Spirit Guides, and Blessed Ones. The slight sound of children's chant was audible. Soon the area was filled with the chant, and all were filled with joy. Elders who had been incapacitated for a generation or more stood straight and raised their arms. Villagers who were blind began to see some light, those who were deaf began to hear, and those who were mentally or physically challenged began to heal. Miracles were seen, and cries were heard from all in the area. Augustin began to shake. Aunewu held tightly upon his hand and gestured for him to bend to listen to him. He said in his ear, "All is well, Father, and you believe wholeheartedly now, yes?" Augustin stood straight, gestured for his son to come close, picked him up, and swung around in a circle. "Yes, yes, son, I do believe," he told his son.

All in the area began to chant loudly. The group stood and united with Augustin and Aunewu. Tears fell freely as all knew they had interacted with the Great Source directly. Lives, minds, and bodies were changed instantly, all by good grace, as they had heard about from the elders for generations. Warec was in the midst of all that was good. He turned to Mabo and Tiao, gestured for a hug, and fell into their unconditional love—he surrendered. To him, this incredible couple was at the top of his list, his utmost favorite people list. Tears flowed freely from him; for the first time in decades, he projected his love out to all. He turned to Quiatua and smiled, bowed at his waist, and asked if she wanted to dance. Quiatua, without hesitation, joined in his bliss. Laughter broke out from all present, and soon all danced.

Massive tears flowed from Katerina. Aunewu grabbed her arms and danced. Katerina reached for all the children, and a circle was formed. She felt like a child; she needed to feel like a child. The children led her out of the center into the village. In the evening air, they gestured for her to sit. To her astonishment, one child communicated with her. The children wanted to know what she knew. With an inquisitive expression on her face, she questioned what was meant. Finally, the child expressed they had seen her and her partner outside in the air with Aunewu. The couple must have explained some things to Aunewu, and now they wanted the information, possibly.

Katerina's mind whirled as she glanced around the area. Suri and villagers traveled toward them and began to sit in the area. Soon a more significant number of people joined. Suri gestured to Katerina, a heart-shaped sign they used between them. Katerina realized these were her moments to share with all present. She closed her eyes, centered, and opened herself, and exhaled slowly. She began communication, when she was a child, her grandfather Pappa G, as she called him, ignited her interest in physics. He took her on many local and distant journeys to professional people who answered their questions. He had studied physics, mathematics, and astrophysics. When it came to physics, she communicated with them, she skyrocketed! One child communicated the question, "What was phy_sics?" A huge smile crossed Katerina's face. She was now in her element as she shared very expressively with facial and body language. The children were in awe. Some propped their elbows on their knees and leaned toward her for all the information. Other children lay on the soft grassed ground and stretched out while they gazed upward to the sky, and some cuddled up to her as close as they could. She explained how all elements humans produce and expel from the Earth affect the atmosphere, and the study of this was ongoing. Katerina looked across at the children and communicated; she had wondered, since the vision and words she had received, what velocity would a Geophysicist have with the group.

A child shot their arm up, as they had seen Aunewu display prior. Suri pointed the child out to Katerina. She looked toward the child and let out a wonderful laugh. The child was adorable, with big brown eyes, thick hair, and a sparkle in their eyes whose light penetrated Katerina's soul. She nodded for the child to communicate. The child shared her thoughts as best she could for her attempt at telepathy. If elements caused by humans changed the at_mos_phere, why would she wonder? She was a genius, right? Katerina laughed out loud and communicated, well perhaps not a genius, yet the girl child had a point; after all, Geophysics was her specialty. With the dawning upon Katerina that the World would need a new basis for everything she learned, she needed to get cracking on everything new.

On that thought, she communicated to the children her appreciation for their love and attention to her explanation of physics and astrophysics. Slowly the children realized their education would continue with Katerina and began to stretch and yawn. One by one, they stood, traveled toward Katerina, offered her a huge hug, traveled to Suri, and gave the same. Suri and Katerina joined, held each other, and marveled at all they had experienced. Katerina acknowledged she needed to contact Koyro; it was time for more pivotal information on her place within the World and during Earth's transition. Suri agreed and realized the same; it was her time to contact her Ascended Master Gaiz for more information. Together they could conquer the amount of information in a quick time. Gaiz and Koyro were not far from the couple's energy and appeared together.

CHAPTER 10

Katerina and Suri felt time vanish as they collaborated diligently with their Ascended Masters and Spirit Guides. The information focused on the change that approached quickly and the consequences on the Earth. The information came from the interaction of several magnificent energies as notes with mathematic equations and explanations. The binders filled quickly as Mabo or Tiao retrieved and stored the books as sacred knowledge with Warec's contributions. Samuel was very attentive to the development of information; he shared thought projections with the Masters as the women worked.

Many species of animals would develop that had been extinct from the Earth. Each species of animal that existed prior had a purpose on the momentum of the Earth. Samuel received visions to recreate sketched species with meticulously written notes that quickly became binders. The information captivated him with the knowledge that he could communicate further at any time with the energies. Zeus, Onyx, and various other animal species approached the women's dwelling from time to time. Samuel, Suri, and Katerina communicated with the animals telepathically as they practiced their abilities. All present remarked on the extraordinary circumstances as they praised the Great Source for the opportunity to live in the moment. The contributions of all were not unnoticed.

Samuel concentrated on the energy to obtain more information toward written notes in herbology. He discovered, to his astonishment, the benefits of seawater, life, and their healing properties. The waters of Earth were abundant with properties harnessed and used with purification methods. Samuel projected thoughts to the Healers and Masters of the polluted masses that floated on and in the seas. He had concerns, and Suri and Katerina had agreed. All three leaned in toward a cloud that manifested. The vision appeared of massive cooperation from the Source and energies as the cleanup of the seas had begun. With collaboration from humans, the cleanup was toward completion. The three sat in astonishment while all took a huge inhale and exhaled slowly. The blessings from the Source were immense.

The horned instrument was heard, and the cloud dissipated as the three gathered their bearings. Samuel wiped his forehead, stretched his arms above his head, stood slowly, and stretched his lengthy body. Suri and Katerina smiled at each other and then to Samuel. All is well, Katerina declared and swung her body toward the dwellings exit and was gone in a flash. Suri and Samuel hugged each other and followed Katerina's path. They had to run to catch Katerina. Her energy glowed a solid golden aura. With footsteps heard behind her, she bent her elbows, and the two engaged her arms with theirs. Side by side, the three entered the village center.

The group gathered with the villagers in a half-circle configuration. Mabo stood tall outside the design with Tiao. Tiao beamed with pride, so much had been conducted from all, and the pride resonated in the area. Mabo generated thoughts that all was well; he received messages that nearby village societies would arrive soon. The compliment to this achievement through the Great Source was that more humans would assist to complete tasks. Within a short time after that, the ones Akaham, Maik, and Omarya visualized would arrive, and healing processes would begin.

With a stir among the gathered, some mumbling could be heard. Mabo raised an arm, and all gathered became silent again. He projected thoughts of no worry as this was great news; the Great Source had great faith all work would be completed. Once completed, all could breathe a sigh of relief and begin to enjoy the company, healings for all gathered, and a sumptuous feast of grown food and eggs supplied would begin. A chant was heard, and the sound became louder as Mabo raised his arms in praise. Tiao gestured the same, and soon all had joined.

The gathered broke from the center and returned to their task. Eusia and Rundda traveled with Mabo and Tiao toward the educational center. All had collaborated diligently with the present villagers. The construction finished, the inside walls were adorned with new tapestry, and beautiful holographic art had been drawn and painted with dye from the local area. The added rooms were with thatched leaf-filled mattresses from wall to wall—designated spaces for needed healings from Eusia and Ascended Healers. Well pleased with the finished product Eusia reached for the bag she carried into the center. She proceeded to pull out an ordained shell and small tied plant-based brush. Rundda exited the center and returned shortly with a fire stick.

Eusia knelt as the others followed. She asked for blessings from the Great Source. As Rundda lit the brush, Eusia reached for more from her bag. Once all four had a lit brush, Eusia instructed them to stand and walk the premises inside and out to smudge the area. Mabo and Tiao gleefully obliged as they danced slowly with sweeping motions. Rundda glanced at Eusia, who stood in silence. A huge smile crossed her face; she winked at Rundda and continued toward the opposite side of the center. Rundda had tears as he watched his beloved in her element. For some reason, he always knew his wife's destiny for greatness. He also obliged with careful steps in sweeping motions and realized he danced slowly.

Aunewu stood with his father, hands locked together as they watched the activity. Augustin lowered his body to his son's level, and a huge smile crossed his face. He told Aunewu "That the time had arrived." Aunewu questioned "Time had arrived for what, Father?" Augustin stood straight, reached, and picked up his son, and walked toward the group as they smudged the exterior of the center's perimeter. When Augustin called Mabo, Mabo turned and questioned if all was well. Augustin communicated to him; yes, indeed, all was well. He requested Mabo to contact his wife, Haou, telepathically. Mabo smiled broadly and motioned for them to enter the center. Due to the request made, Mabo communicated with the others. The other three gathered the materials and joined them in the center of the building.

Aunewu was thrilled to have his father ask Mabo to communicate with his mother: he hoped his mother could join them. For precisely what to join in, he was not sure. Eusia understood the velocity of the moment as she reached for the crystals on the table. Augustin had an issue with telepathic communications, as Aunewu's Ascended Master Dyne, appeared. He beamed with such love and light. Dyne materialized a cloud as Aunewu saw a form appear. Aunewu's face lit brighter than the sun, his aura turned violet, and he bowed at his waist. His mother, Haou, was peaceful as she sat in meditation and present. Augustin's eyes clouded, tears formed; he fought back the urge to reach for her, fearing the cloud would dissipate. Dyne made a gesture, and Haou opened her heart, mind, and soul. A witnessed golden color mixed with violet surrounded her form.

Rundda knelt at the time, followed by Tiao, Mabo, Augustin, and Aunewu. Dyne gestured for Augustin to communicate with Haou verbally if more comfortable. Haou would receive the message in a short time. Augustin choked up at the opportunity, closed his eyes, inhaled deeply, and exhaled slowly. Then, he communicated out loud to his beloved in his native language. When young people recognized their monumental journey of growth and connection with "Ahnah," their most excellent spirit, a wonderful ritual took place in their culture. A short time passed, and energy resonated; all was well, and Haou agreed. She felt the time had arrived before the journey her son and husband were on together. Love, light, and soft chimes of musical instruments were audible.

All present bowed at their waist, joined by Dyne for the sacred moment, and the Great Source was aware. Haou sent energy toward all; she wished to be present after discussing a suitable time when other children in the village could join Aunewu on the monumental occasion. Aunewu beamed with light and wanted all children to join him. He felt a kinship with the village, especially all the children. Again, Haou sent energy; she was available when contacted again. The cloud disappeared slowly, along with the sound of music. Mabo stood slowly, gained his bearings, and gestured for everyone to join him. Dyne's energy, pleased with the progress, dissipated slowly.

Eusia and Tiao smiled broadly at all gathered. Eusia raised the crystals in her hands, gleaming light with their colors. Tiao would suggest a time for the children to collect after the evening feast to the village elders. Aunewu felt a rush of cool air cross his body; he felt lighter and knew his mother had sent him love. Aunewu grabbed his father's hands, and Augustin felt the love from his mother at once. He wiped tears from his eyes and bowed at his waist to all present. Mabo appointed until later; all should return to their task. All left the center and went ahead to their task.

Again, before dusk, after the sound of the horned instrument and a grand caravan of horses, carts, and wagons came on the horizon. Most villagers and the group gathered in the center of the village. Some people became delayed as they finished securing animals and food for the feast. Finally, the caravan came closer, and Quiatua waved excitedly toward all as she blew a kiss toward Saib and Majestic. Aunewu released the bunched vegetables he held onto the center table and asked permission to greet them. With a gleam in his eye, Augustin granted permission. Aunewu waved to the other children to join in the greeting. With enthusiasm, the children broke from their stance and all hopped, skipped, jumped, and ran toward the outskirts of the village. The joy of welcome oozed from their bodies as Saib slowed the caravan.

Saib communicated appreciation for such a wonderful welcome as he was quick to issue caution around the weary horses and other livestock from the journey. Children, elders, and adults peeked out the wagons and carts toward the excitement. Broad smiles appeared, and they felt love from the children toward the caravan. The procession moved slowly toward the center. Mabo and Tiao stood nearby the entrance to livestock pens and a campsite area for the carts and wagons. The group and villagers aided with the organization of the arranged site. A tall man exited the last carriage in the procession and stretched his body to its full length as he reached his hand toward the rear of the cart. An adorned elder exited the cart, and the tall man assisted him to stand on his feet.

Upon sight of the elder, Mabo knelt and bowed. All others joined in this tribute, for they understood the elder was of great status. The elder reached for his staff provided to him by the man who supported his waist. The elder gestured, saying in his native tongue: all is well and for all to join him in praise. All raised their bodies at their waist, raised their arms high, and joined in recognition of the Great Source. The visitor's journey was a success, and all gathered showed their appreciation. Mabo stood, gathered his bearings, and introduced the tall man as his brother, Zau, and the elder as their grandfather, Usa. All three men hugged, and after explaining the monumental occasion of ceremony for the children, Usa communicated he would be honored to deliver the words. The honor was upon all gathered as Usa was a high priest.

CHAPTER 11

While the celebration took place with Usa and the children, Akaham and Maik appeared. The honor was theirs as not for generations had they seen this number of children recognized in their walk of faith with the Great Source. With sincerity, the children realized, on their own time, their worth on the Earth. So many more generations would recognize it as well in a short time. Children bowed toward Usa, Akaham, and Maik; they knew their lifestyle had been ushered onto the Earth. The children had pride, abundant light, and love as they realized the magnitude of the moments.

Several days had passed when the sound of the horned instrument was heard. All gathered in the center of the village. Mabo and Tiao stood with such pride. They looked at the village and its transformation and the camp nearby villagers had taken for the events to unfold. Mabo raised his arms in a gesture toward the Great Source and began a blessing request. Mabo addressed all present and communicated the arrival of the individuals the elders foresaw would arrive that day. Those individuals would be in a significant number. The individuals would be of the territorial war zones, as said earlier. Murmurs were heard from those gathered.

The Ascended Masters of the group appeared. All those gathered bowed in respect; they had become accustomed to the visits and felt honored to be in the presence of the Masters. The Masters generated great care, love, and light for all gathered. The transformed village was beyond belief as it gleamed from the dawn light as the sun ascended in the sky. All was well, Dyne, Aunewu's Ascended Master, communicated to all. He appointed the Great Source in all their infinite wisdom and was well pleased with the immeasurable efforts of all who had gathered and completed their task. Peluan, Eusia's Ascended Master, raised his energy as some of the Blessed Ones arranged in the area around those gathered. Yallow, Warec's Ascended Master, generated his power as a light, sun-filled rain fell upon the location.

The children and Aunewu wanted to prance, run and jump in the rain. Formli, Mabo's Ascended Master, gestured for the children to stand at their places. With love she generated, all children would play in the rain later. The children bowed at her presence and settled in their places. Luna, Samuel's Ascended Master, communicated the moment had arrived. Koyro, Gaiz, and Baou—Katerina, Suri, and Quiatua's Ascended Masters, bowed when the horses and carts were visible on the outskirts of the village.

Akaham and Maik appeared and communicated; yes, all was well. The time was correct for all the moments that had come and passed with such vigor and talent to prepare the village. Those who had aided in the transformation were ready to help individuals upon arriving at the center. Maik expanded her energy to those individuals as they came. Akaham bowed as they entered the center of the village. All who were present took his lead and bowed upon their arrival. The Blessed Ones generated a low hum vibration while Spirit Guides appeared. The Great Source sent more Blessed Ones, and all felt the grace that supported the moment. Akaham sent energy to all present who would begin a procession toward the educational center and aid the individuals with the journey.

Children did not hesitate to the carts while they extended their hands and arms toward people when they exited the carts. Smiles beamed on their faces, and they felt a part of the expansion of time and care. Adults and elders present began at a slow pace, not rushing the people who exited from the carts. The numbers of people were significant, as communicated earlier. Young babies, mothers, families, elders, fathers, sons and daughters, and some random animals were all met with love, light, caring hands, and arms. Some people recoiled during such interactions as expected.

However, these people were met by a Blessed One, taller than life, serene in presence, light-filled them with love, and the people soon realized they were in the best place. Slowly the procession moved toward and around the educational center.

Once all settled, Eusia proceeded to kneel and pray. All others who could do so found their place, and a moment was shared with all. Two Blessed Ones then lifted Eusia. All in the area could see her, and she began with a bow in all four directions. She opened her mind, heart, and spirit as she looked at everyone gathered. She prayed for everyone in attendance to assist her with all those who needed help. A grand washing of all souls was to take place. No one present had to fear being taken advantage of, maimed, or killed. All people who had arrived looked bewildered at the notion that such a time had come, such a place existed, and such a wonderful spirit had rescued them. Tears fell among some present. Others wanted to sit and settle in, bathe in the sun, the love, and the light.

Eusia communicated for all in dire situations and needed attention to continue inside the center. Those who could sit and bathe in love and light and be restored outside the center should be allowed. People would be fed and given plenty of clean water, and visible wounds be cared for by all who could aid. She and others would gain much information inside the center and administer more profound healings. She communicated that all who were able and willing to experience the teachings would be welcomed soon. As she had shared with Peluan prior, all humans needed this knowledge. She and the others were not privileged, just the selected ones to aid, and teachings would go from one to another. Once she had completed her thoughts, the Blessed Ones lowered her to the ground. Eusia coupled Rundda's hands with hers. She kissed him on his cheek, turned, and bowed at her waist before entering the center.

Warec held a man up by his waist with the man's arm over his shoulder, who had been severely beaten. He inhaled and exhaled slowly. He took in the moment and smiled at the man as others around him drew closer. Formli appeared and communicated to Warec; well done, good to inhale and exhale. You will see a gamut of health issues. The men who closed in were members of the man's troop. The man was their captain, and he had been beaten and burned in areas of his body under clothing not seen. The men were concerned about his well-being. Warec communicated to

Formli to acknowledge to the men all was well and they needed to stay close by outside the center. The villagers would address the men's visible wounds. Communication was understood; the men nodded toward Warec and saluted toward their captain. Warec proceeded slowly with the man toward and entered the center.

Samuel instinctively grabbed the video recorder as some children approached him with theirs in hand. The smile on Samuel's face invited the children to join as they entered the center. Spirit Guides acknowledged the children as they were separated toward other areas of the center and stood nearby the adjacent rooms. Katerina escorted children who could walk inside the center, some with bandages on their heads, others with arms in a sling; a few used a crutch- fashioned branch to aid their walk. Suri's heart swelled when she saw the care Katerina focused on with the children as they assisted them to sit on thatched leaf- filled pads. Quiatua, accompanied by Azna, smiled as her eyes adjusted to the light inside the center. She had escorted several malnourished adults. The adults were helped to the side of the center by Azna and other Guides. Quiatua exited the center to retrieve more people in dire need.

Aunewu and Augustin wasted no delay in helping women with infants and children under the age of one. They found villagers as Aunewu communicated thoughts these people needed food, clean water, and bathing. At the nearby camp area, he and his father would help. Some people realized they needed aid in the camp, and their injuries were minor; they were hungry, dehydrated, and needed rest. The nearby villagers at the camp walked toward and received them with open hearts, minds, spirits, and arms. A few people collapsed into the arms of the men and women. Children mingled around and chose where they could best help. Dyne, Aunewu's Ascended Master, appeared and gleamed with a brightness some people had to shade their eyes. They did not realize the power was healing light from the Great Source. Dyne communicated with Aunewu; well done, and keep the energy blessings generated toward all in the area. Aunewu smiled and saluted Dyne, who graciously nodded energy toward him and his father.

Mabo and Tiao held one another by the waist, turned toward each other, and hugged. The vision they had received had been proven before them. Tiao adjusted the ornamented pin on Mabo, patted the emblem, and kissed Mabo on his cheek. Mabo bowed at his waist and gestured his arm toward the center's entrance as to him, Tiao was his queen, his beloved. She entered the center first, and both squinted as their eyes adjusted to the light. Such energy generated from the center out toward the village and people, Mabo and Tiao gripped each other to gain their bearing. They saw Ascended Masters, Spirit Guides, and Ascended Healers work in tandem with the people, the villagers, and the group. They winked at each other and jumped into action.

Eusia kept all in the center under direction with help from the Masters and Healers, much to her relief. The healings began when all in need of aid settled. The energy became slower, the heartbeats of all present slowed, thought processes cleared, and the air became clear from traces of negativity experienced. Akaham and Maik appeared in the area, whose energy bowed toward Eusia. She felt a flush run across the core of her being; she closed her eyes, inhaled deeply, and exhaled slowly. She knew the size of the moments ahead for all present. Surprisingly to her, she began with a chant, as a slow drumbeat began from somewhere nearby, the hum of Blessed Ones resonated in the area, and those in need of aid inside and outside fell quickly to sleep. As explained by Peluan prior, this was so all could experience peace with rest and not have anxiety about the healing.

Rundda approached Eusia and sounded a small gong instrument. Eusia chose crystals from the table and instructed nearby children to manage with care and go toward the four directions and face outwards toward the wall. The children, as their smiles beamed, did as instructed. Eusia retrieved lighted tied bundles of herbs and then handed one each to the available group members. As she motioned for Samuel to participate in the ritual, he looked bewildered. Rundda retrieved the video recorder and continued the recording of events. The group members were instructed to walk the exterior perimeter of the center, village, and camp area quietly in reflection, upon completion, return and enter the center. Eusia then turned toward Akaham and Maik, who instructed the Healers in their infinite abilities to begin the healings within the center, the village, and the camp area.

All the group, villagers, and those who came to help felt the light mist of water. The mist, hum, drumbeat, crystals, and lite herbs were for purification. The air became more lightweight, and the energy became quickened. The comfort of all present was of great concern to the Great Source. Azna instructed the children who stood in the four directions to turn toward the center and become comfortable as the Healers began to work. All present received communicated instructions to whom needed what type of care, prayer, cleansings with water and oils supplied by the Masters, and clean bandages. Meticulous detail was given to the people and their minds, bodies, and spirits. While they slept, they did not know what had maneuvered around for them.

Hours past in a blink of an eye. The people who had arrived received such care. Samuel was beside himself in tears. He was not the only one seen to wipe away wells of tears from his eyes. So many people, such trauma, and such tragic events that brought these people to this point. Some had injuries so developed that he wondered how they could have withstood such an injustice. The ages range from very young to elders who should be respected, not injured. How many people from that territory had yet to make the journey, let alone the exit of that area? Luna, his Ascended Master, appeared and gleamed with light. She communicated that all was well; those who did not journey or exit the area were with the Blessed Ones. The Ones had instructions from Great Source to cocoon the peoples' spirits so that they could heal for eternity: never would they have to repeat another lifetime. The people would be Ascended Masters or Healers.

Some people transitioned peacefully toward the light which illuminated the center. Those spirits met a Blessed One and were escorted directly to the Great Source. Their human body was retrieved, respectively, placed on thatched stretchers, and removed from the center for last ceremony rites. Great Source granted the ones connected to the spirit a blessing to meet them one last time and know all was well during the sleep state. Those awake during the healing were astounded by the beauty and peace in the moment.

Warec worked nearby the captain, so consumed by hope the man would heal, recover and see the faces of the men in the troop again. He did not realize Maik had joined the man. She bent her energy toward him and caught Warec off guard when he felt a sharp breeze between them. Startled, he looked up to see Maik in her complete form as she lifted the man, blew into his nostrils, and lowered him toward his mat. Pleased with her effort, she straightened her form, turned toward Warec, and sent energy; all was well, and the man would see his men again.

The energy shifted as the Masters and Healers pulled back toward the side walls and directed their thoughts toward Eusia. Samuel and the children had recorded all events and bowed at their waist toward Eusia in the center of the area. She realized the velocity of all and the experience. Unsure, she wondered why others bowed toward her; instead, she felt blessed to be in their presence. Eusia motioned for the cameras to continue recording the events, for Rundda to sound the gong, and for those present to kneel to receive a message. A cloud appeared as the energy of the Great Source was felt by all. Well pleased with the efforts, care, and education, the Great Source illuminated the cloud. The cloud sent the energy of love, light, and care toward all who had assisted. When the cloud dissipated, thoughts were generated that the sleeping ones were to awaken in a short time.

As those awoke, they discovered such peace throughout their being. The illuminated light above them turned a gold color. They could sit up with aid, recover, and feel hunger for food and nourishment. Some were astonished by their learned knowledge after the sleep state; they were eager to communicate what happened. Jumbled thoughts were projected, murmurs were heard, and the shuffle of people in their attempts to stand filled the air. Akaham and Maik generated thoughts to slow down, sit down, and take the energy internally. The healing was to continue throughout the next several hours as they received food and nourishment outside of the center. Eusia motioned to Rundda, and the gong sounded. The group, villagers, and those who came to help walked together toward the awoken ones and aided in their departure from the center.

People outside the center were astonished to see those who exited without the same ailments as when they entered. Some came to the aid of those who left, and others communicated when would be their turn for the events that appeared to have healed the others. Mabo and Tiao exited the center and expressed there would be more sessions as time passed. To explain to those in need, those who aided those who left the center, needed some recovery as well, was heartbreaking but necessary. A feast was planned, and the children needed to prance, run and jump.

Tiao communicated that all the children who participated in the aid were so wonderful and patient they needed some fun time. All who had approached the couple understood, smiled and nodded, turned, and settled in their areas. Sunshine lit the space as light rain fell, and the children began to run, dance and play.

CHAPTER 12

Great Source was well pleased, and the rain was a gift to all in the area. The children's energy was contagious, and the Great Source was delighted for the joy, the well-being of all, the work completed in tandem among all, and for those who needed rest received this most of all as they healed. For Great Source, there was no essence of time. Their energy could be bilocal and concentrated on several events Worldwide simultaneously. Their power was all-knowing, especially when Ascended Masters and Healers, Spirit Guides, and Power Animals called out questions or in need and response to their instructions.

Omarya was given a message from several Blessed Ones about the celebration. Deep respect and energy were sent to all who participated. However, the adjustment to the following lifestyle could have been smoother. Omarya had seen the apparent effects of the Earth's transition. For most humans, day-to-day living had come to a crawl. Most did not understand what had happened, and much anxiety also came. Some humans stated and felt they were to experience another global pandemic. Memories flooded back to most humans when the whole World shut down and when previous frivolous spending on materialistic items seemed wasted. Yet some humans had turned another corner and advanced their spending on more trinkets or unconventional items bought due to no self-restraint or became greedy.

Humans had advanced greater in that short time than during their entire lifetime. Most humans had not, however. Some humans considered the pivotal turn of events to be wrath. The question on most humans' minds was wrath from what or whom? Omarya had an earlier life in a country during a war. He reflected on the energy that felt like wrath. Many humans then considered the end of time coming upon Earth. Many of those humans issued their resolution, and they took their own lives. He understood that at times of dismay, humans either reverted within themselves, came out fighting, or went to war. His energy called for more messages to reach the human population sooner. His power concentration brought forth Akaham and Maik from the Great Source.

The thought process began between the trio with Omarya. He projected different observations where some humans were weak, untrusting, and unable to initiate positive thoughts out to the World. He questioned if other energies had seen the same. How could aid be quickened before more humans surrendered to negative thoughts and actions? Was Great Source to put out messages at a rapid pace? If so, when? Akaham generated ideas the human species needed to understand to heal themselves and their lives; first, they needed to turn their selfish attention to healing the World's land, seas, and sky. Maik communicated no lack of humans knew of this transition ahead of the actual event. These humans have generated energy for decades and have flourished at present. Those humans who saw their efforts began to complement the accompanied lifestyle.

Omarya's energy contemplated the thoughts shared. His energy became disturbed while both Maik and Akaham recognized the signs of his discomfort. A Blessed One appeared, sent directly from Great Source with a message. The message the Blessed One delivered was of great comfort to all present. A cloud formed, and a vision appeared. The image depicted the humans on Earth as they no longer struggled with the onset of the Earth's transition. The humans had gained their knowledge and belief system. The change startled most humans. When the next internet released the vision, words, and workings of the chosen seven individuals' efforts, the mindset of the humans switched. Most humans became aware of their actions, lack of activities, thought processes, and physical, mental, emotional, and spiritual bodies.

Some humans' lifetimes were spent with immense struggles to survive, fighting to provide food and water for themselves, their children, and their elders. These humans were the first to receive such nutrition from the staples released during the transition. These humans praised the efforts of others to provide, praised the One who had aided, advanced their knowledge, or deepened their belief system with the Great Source. All witnessed the humans and species released from territorial war areas, oppressive leaders or familial people, taken from their homelands and placed in bondage as they fell toward the Earth. Their cries and praise rocked their bodies; they needed substance from the One who helped release them. They continued or developed an in-depth belief system with the Great Source.

Humans who were interested in only their day-to-day lifestyles became more aware of the outer influences around the World. Their awareness shifted toward abundant thought processes for all inhabitants of the Earth. The serenity they felt spread outwards in their immediate area, spreading further around the World. The humans became more like-minded because of the efforts. In the thought process that all humans were created equal, all species on the planet had a purpose, the seas, land, and air should remain pure and not overexploited, no human denied the main staples of nutrients, and no plant life strangled from their right to produce. The list of reckoning grew longer as more humans realized the velocity of human action or lack of action had placed on their beloved Mother Earth.

How could humans aid toward or replace what they had deprived or taken from Mother Earth? Humans who had felt the abuse of societies toward Mother Earth now rallied in the dawning of the new thought process. The next internet flourished with positive affirmations daily, video-recorded services and words, sketches, paintings, and meditation practices, while recorded healings were within reach to all humans. To echo what the Great Source had allowed on the Earth for centuries: to love, honor, and adore the planet, and She will give back to you three- folds; was within a human's spiritual reach and at their fingertips, spread like wildfire Worldwide. Mother Earth sighed when the relief of much pent-up energy had released Her to do what She had always done: produce, lighten the load for humans, and supply clean water, air, and staples.

Omarya's energy also sighed with relief. His energy was being depleted from negativity passed onto him through human thoughts. His power had taken on the brunt of the humans' anxiety and needed a recuperation time. Maik, without hesitation, gestured to the Blessed One, who dissipated after that. Omarya's energy recognized the need yet wanted to maintain the honor bestowed. To see the Masters, Guides, Blessed Ones, and the Great Source continue their efforts toward the great transition. Maik projected thoughts of Omarya's energy in a cocoon state that the revitalization his energy needed would restore his thought process, wipe negativity, and the cause-effect would be the reset. Akaham produced a thought process that also appointed the great transition of the humans' partaking. That Omarya could rest, restore and release the negativity without losing the time, the honor, or the loss of witnessed events.

The Blessed One appeared, the Great Source agreed to the request, and, without further excitement, when Omarya signaled the cocoon state would be in effect. The Great Source had appointed that any spirit that needed the reset and whose energy had worked diligently granted the same. Others would be aligned to continue the task with the humans. Akaham projected thoughts that while Omarya recuperated his energy, others would also do the same. The undertaking of the Earth's transition was to be an overhaul for the spirit world as well, and all would eventually take part. Easing Omarya's energy, Akaham added Omarya's energy would exemplify by example to all spirits; rest, recovery, and reset were all good and considered necessary from the Great Source. Omarya's energy faded into a lighter state and acknowledged the appreciation toward all present and the Great Source.

CHAPTER 13

Luna, Samuel's Ascended Master, had introduced him and the numerous children to what the Great Source considered the 'next internet.' The group, the villagers, and the guests were astonished. Most of the group knew about the internet, yet it had a new essence upon its delivery. Positive thoughts were generated from devices placed on the center of the village tables by the Ascended Masters. Some humans recoiled in fear or disbelief as they had never seen or experienced such things. Luna gestured toward Samuel, who then walked toward a thatched chair and sat. The children sat in wild wonder, what was to take place, what were they all immersed in, and were they so honored to be present at the exact moment when all would be explained?

Indeed, they were, as Azna, Quiatua's Spirit Guide, projected as her form took shape and she leaned toward the children and Samuel. Azna continued instruction for those present and with children nearby the devices. Her patience and love resonated as the high and bright yellow light she emitted enveloped all in the area. She communicated the device's name and operation ability slowly to all. She gestured toward the sky when she came to the part where all information added and uploaded to the instruments would go nowhere. However, she said the information added would go somewhere. One child imitated Aunewu's earlier gestures and raised his arm high. Azna, pleased with the boy's sincere expression, granted permission to communicate.

The boy, known as Yao, emitted colors of yellow toward all in the area. He felt honored to communicate with all others. Yao transmitted, the information went into the at_mos_phere with an excellent grin for the accomplishment he had learned through Suri and Katerina. Both women beamed with gratitude toward Yao and the children. They both formed the heart sign toward the children, who returned the same sign with grins and giggles. Azna commenced her instructions with a loving hug toward Yao and the children. The children gleamed different colors. Parents and elders in the area raised their arms in praise. Finally, Azna communicated atmosphere was near the site, yes, correct. The information is transferred toward a web-type structure. The children's eyes darted anxiously around the area and skywards. Some squinted to see the web-type system.

Azna waved toward the sky, and slowly the illuminated web appeared. All gathered were astounded by the prior unseen web. Some in the group smiled and projected loving thoughts that all was well. The web had been there all along, never visible until that moment. Azna continued her instructions. The children with recorded devices were to sit with Samuel and learn. The hustle was profound as the Ascended Masters and Guides helped the closest children to thatched chairs. Great joy was evident in the children's spirits. Once settled, Azna gestured toward Samuel, who was to commence with the instructions.

Peluan, Eusia's Ascended Master, appeared and produced thoughts of the ones who had arrived and needed healing to enter the educational center slowly. The ones who needed further rest were welcomed to lay on the furnished mats in the adjacent rooms. The slow progression began toward the center while parents and elders gave the concern expressions 'be on your best behavior' to the children who awaited their time for a device. The children shared their respect toward the matter as some bowed their heads toward their loved ones. Dyne, Aunewu's Ascended Master, gestured toward the parents and elders; all was well, and they would receive a report if any issues arose. All the children bowed their heads toward Dyne with great respect, and some generated thoughts, as this education was too interesting to miss!

The group, minus Samuel, went toward the center, bowed, and entered. Another healing session was upon them; every time they entered and aided, they received healing energy as well. Usa, Mabo's grand elder, was aided by Zau and Tiao into the center, where a significant, thatched chair was placed for him. Eusia turned toward Quiatua, smiled, and gestured for her to join. Quiatua felt so honored she had to gain bearings as she gripped Katerina's arm for support. Katerina patted her hand and, with Quiatua, proceeded toward Eusia; when she went to return to her place, she also was welcomed. Eusia gestured toward all others of the group, with Suri and Rundda joining. Mabo approached the group, asked for the blessings of the Great Source and bowed toward the group. The healing began when the illuminated light entered the center of the space. Eusia reached for the tied brush, Mabo lit the brush, and Eusia handed one to each member. Each walked the inside perimeter of the center as they slowly swayed, a soft drumbeat was audible. Soft hums were heard from the Blessed Ones as a cloud appeared.

The Great Source emanated from the cloud; all was well. The progress seen pleased them, and everyone in the area would receive a gift after the healing. Some humans bowed, others raised their arms, and praise was heard from all inside and outside the center. The center's energy changed slowly, and the healing began as the cloud dissipated. Eusia passed each member a crystal upon their return to the table. Mabo selected Aunewu, Augustin, Warec, and Rundda to stand in the four directions. Koyro, Katerina's Ascended Master, appeared and issued for all those present for the healing to lay in comfort, close their eyes, inhale and exhale slowly, and visualize the green light of healing, which encompassed them. Once settled, Koyro instructed all in the area this was the first task toward self-healing meditation. Koyro produced thoughts all humans had this innate ability toward self-healing; they only needed to be reminded.

Koyro nodded toward Eusia, who instructed those in the group to join her. She gathered the crystals and placed them on the tabletop as they illuminated their colors toward the yellow light in the center. Eusia then gestured for the group to mimic her action. She turned and bowed toward the four directions, as did the group. She knelt and raised her arms in praise of the Great Source, as did the group. She stood, turned toward all in the center, bowed, and welcomed the love, healing, and reset for the humans in the center, as did the group. The air filled with a mist of colors and descended toward all in the center. The group felt the immediate effects as they reached to grip each other to gain their bearings. The subtle and slow progression of the healing was seen. Eusia's smile was broad, and she gestured to the group to retrieve a crystal, walk the area where possible and to fan the crystal where energy was called.

The group did as instructed. Some concentrated so deeply their Ascended Master had to inject, to slow the thought process, be in the moment; the energy would not be read if hurried. Then, one by one, the members saw when the crystal came toward a human and summoned closer. To their astonishment, they had no choice but to follow the energy. The experience was immense to each of them, and there was no denial; the power was needed, and they were needed and required to conduct the phenomenon that existed at the moment. Rundda smiled toward Eusia, who beamed her light toward him, for he had seen this through his beloved on many occasions: now, he experienced the energy firsthand. All the time, the power generated from the crystal was so serene, so treasured, and so clear of the intention the overflow was felt by all in the area.

The hours felt like they moved at a few blinks of the eye. The fully welcomed subtle energy of the crystals, sacred light from the Great Source, the burnt brush, and the concentration from the group, had most humans resonate with the power around the center. The total velocity of the witnessed event did not fall short of any human involvement. Some restless humans began to sit up slowly, open their eyes, and breathe slowly, taking in the actions and love generated for all. Eusia stood next to Usa, who reached for her hand. She waved toward the others to gather at the table. When all assembled, Eusia patted Usa's hand, bowed her head toward him and released her hand. He felt honored to be in the wonderful woman's presence and well-loved. As more humans realized the healing had connected them to the present, they regained consciousness, sat up, and breathed slowly as they opened their eyes.

Yellow, Warec's Ascended Master, appeared and gestured well done to all present. He motioned for Warec to move toward Eusia and Rundda. Warec did as instructed as Eusia reached to uncover items on the table. The same emblem worn by Mabo and Eusia was present, and she reached for one, walked closer toward Warec, smiled at him, and pinned the emblem onto his chest above his heart on his clothing. Warec felt so honored, he reached for Eusia's hand and asked with eyes for permission to place an affectionate kiss upon the top, she nodded, and Warec continued. When he released her hand to continue to the next person, Warec whipped tears from his eyes as he bowed toward Eusia and Mabo. Eusia continued the same for Quiatua, Katerina, Suri, Rundda, Aunewu, and Augustin, who blushed when he received his emblem. She gently touched Aunewu's shoulder and gestured for him to retrieve Samuel.

All present were unsure what had occurred yet understood something so magnificent was theirs to have seen. Samuel entered the center as he was pulled by the hand from the very excited Aunewu. Who had such scrambled thoughts, Samuel could only make out from him that he was needed in the center. Samuel's eyes had to adjust to the brilliance within the center. When he felt out of balance, Luna, his Ascended Master, aided him toward the table. He realized outstanding events had occurred as he noticed the symbol pinned to all others present. Eusia reached for him to move closer and pinned the emblem above his heart on his clothing. With the final member pinned, Usa stood with aid, and Mabo, Tiao, and Eusia bowed toward the members. The newly pinned members returned the bow toward the four and knelt on their knees while prayers were softly heard.

Time stood still as a cloud appeared. Maik, Akaham, and the spiritually rested Omarya began to form. Eusia prayed over all present, the crystals, burnt brush, and several other items on the table. Once she finished her prayer, Mabo gestured for all in the center to aid others in need with their mats and continue to exit toward the village center. The trio of spirits in their magnificent forms followed the last ones to leave toward the village center. Mabo gestured that everyone gathered should find a comfortable place. The trio was present in the center so all could see their messages. As the group members and villagers aided those needing comfort and some clean water, Maik projected her thoughts first.

Maik began with her great admiration for all those gathered, for the incredible kindness of the villagers, the members of the group, and most all, the Great Source for their steadfast belief in all humans. Akaham projected his thoughts next with the same admiration and added the humans present were blessed beyond what their minds could perceive. Omarya cast his thoughts with a visualization next. The exact visualization he had received before his cocoon. Where all was indeed well, the Earth had continued its revolution in the universe and around the sun, the seas cleared from pollution, the air cleaner as the smog had lifted, and various negative political agendas worldwide dissolved. While human, plant life, and animals roamed free in harmony, where no mortal fear of retaliation was present. Audible sounds of sighs were heard, some present lifted their arms skyward, and praise was heard.

The Blessed Ones appeared, and a soft drumbeat was audible. The hum the humans were so pleased to hear was present, and the flute sound was heard. All present in the area bowed as Omarya produced thoughts that all had received the same healing ability that Eusia was familiar with during her lifetime. Some humans were astounded by the realization of this responsibility. Would their lives be forever changed? Could they manage such energy? Would they crumble under pressure to deliver so elegantly as Eusia had done with their healings? On the contrary, Omarya appointed, they would be slow to acquire the ability yet would come to appreciate the energy as they received the privileged esteem. Not esteem they would hold only for themselves; they were to meditate on their journey to their homelands, they would realize upon arrival in their regions, other humans would seek them. Some would travel great distances with others who bade for their help. All the staples would be supplied upon their arrival. They and the others would not perish.

CHAPTER 14

As the realization of the progress occurred to all present, some humans reached for one another, and others sat astounded. Their freedom, health, and right to live life fully were restored. What a liberating moment for the 'guest.' The villagers felt honored to have partaken in the events, and the group members felt honored but a sense of loss at the same time. They began with weeks of preparation for the journey and acclimated upon arriving at this phenomenal place reserved for such a transition. They had learned and experienced so much more and needed to travel toward their homelands now: most members wanted to stay.

Akaham recognized the awareness descending upon the group as his energy turned toward them. He projected thoughts outward to all in the area. He clarified that the chosen seven individuals and their companions would be Ambassadors for each continent with direct access to Akaham and Maik. He explained that reason alone was enough for the seven individuals to travel to this sacred and freed land. The instructions, education, learning, and work completed in tandem with all in the area was teaching the seven humans beyond their greatest expectations for themselves. One by one, the group glanced at one another, and all agreed as they nodded their heads toward each other. Each of them knew they would have never experienced anything to this extent without one another in unison.

Maik injected her thoughts into the process. The seven humans would stand for all the procedures that had become their daily existence since their arrival. The care, sharing of knowledge and skills, the healing abilities, the diversity of multi- cultures and humans, and the growing of plants, herbs, and tree life and not limited to the growth of knowledge alongside the animal kingdom. She radiated golden light direct from the Great Source to all in the area, for she knew as did the Blessed Ones, Omarya, Akaham, the Ascended Masters and Healers, the Spirit Guides, and the Great Source that none of the preceding events would have taken place without the incredible humans that dwelled at this place. Mabo, Tiao, Zau, Usa, and their people bowed toward Maik; the honor was theirs to have such a transition of the Earth become their way of life. Maik explained that all these humans had lived through generations knowing Great Source had higher intentions for them. They and their land were the heartbeats of Mother Earth.

Usa raised his arms and faced skyward. In his native language, he thanked Mother Earth for the honor of everyone in the area. He raised a prayer toward the Great Source and thanked them also. He asked that all the animal kingdom genuinely know no fear from or toward humankind. All species of the land could live as one, and that aid was available when called upon for the animal kingdom. The atmosphere, he had gathered from the children who admired Katerina and Suri so highly, remain clean of pollution, and was clear of any negativity. The seas and land water remain clean compared to the earlier state due to human pollutants and abuse. He settled into the grand thatched chair and appeared to pray intensely.

The spirits gathered bowed toward Usa, for they knew he and his grand elders had recited for generations this time of the World would arrive. Usa saw this phenomenon. Usa as a human was one of the precious few. As a spirit, he rode a white stallion toward his grand elders onto the Other Side. Akaham surrounded the grand elder with golden light, laid his energy upon him, and bid Usa farewell as he raised his power skyward to thank Great Source for retrieving one of the Grand Ones. All who gathered realized slowly that the spirit of Usa had transitioned. Some raised their arms in prayer, and some whipped tears from their eyes. Some gestured a blown kiss skyward. All knew Usa had finished what he had come to do: take part and usher in the new lifestyle on Earth. Mabo, Zau, and all others offered praise to Usa.

Akaham gestured toward the emblem of the group. His thought processes appointed that the symbol was of honor and trust. The Great Source visualized these seven individuals, and their companions were to be considered the Ambassadors. Gasps of astonishment were heard. Could this be so? Did the area villagers, the 'guest,' and the spirit world witness a phenomenon beyond compare? Yes, Akaham continued, all present were witness to such, the Ambassadors as so considered from this point forward, were not of hierarchy, yet were of atonement. The expression mystified some humans in the area, and others bowed their heads toward the group. All in the group seemed uncomfortable by the admiration and words. Maik injected her thoughts into the process, and this, too, shall come in time for all these individuals in the group. Much will be processed as human time continues. The group members were to hold themselves in high esteem, not allowing negativity to dictate their thoughts and actions. A tall order indeed!

Akaham completed the thought process with a visualization. For health and healing questions and aid, all gathered would acclimate toward the new devices. As time continued, those present would begin to research and practice their abilities with others; however, if one struggled, they could always reach one of the Ambassadors and their companions via the next internet. To calm the unease, Akaham reminded those present all were in dire need of aid; they now had the same ability to help. Which needed concentration and practice; however, you were never alone. The group members beamed with golden light, and each knew how feeling alone felt. Never was there a need for these feelings again. Questions in regard to herbs and animal kingdom, contact would be with Samuel and Warec. Stunned at this, both men glanced at each other, realized the scope of the events, and graciously nodded toward the other.

For health and healing help, Eusia and Rundda first, then all others in the group. Quiatua released an unavoidable shrill which she tried to stifle unsuccessfully. Then cheers from all in the area rose, and Quiatua shyly bowed her head toward all. She could only imagine the long-range effects of the transition Worldwide, and she was fully present for every moment! Akaham acknowledged Quiatua and the excitement in the air as he continued. For the Earth and atmospheric conditions, questions toward knowledge and aid in these areas and mathematical questions and needed equations would go to Katerina and Suri. Akaham explained these two women were top of their fields. Their assistance was immense during this journey in more ways than ever imagined.

If, for some reason, they had little or no information, they were the type of humans who would receive aid from others and relay the same to those who asked. These women were always available for the higher good, and others should take advantage of their knowledge and now written word, which would appear on the following internet soon. Katerina and Suri reached for each other's hand, glanced at each other and realized the extent of the moment. They had worked side by side since their 'aha moment' after arrival. Their efforts were compiled and ready for upload for the World's reference, and the WOW moment resonated between them as they gripped each other's hand tighter and bowed toward Akaham.

Maik injected with loving expression toward Mabo, Tiao, and Zau with the transition of Usa, and the honor was theirs and the village people to care of 'his last wishes.' As Zau understood the meaning and had prepared before the journey, Usa would be honored with all present and before departure. Maik bowed her energy toward Zau. He was a remarkable human who took care of so many matters for so many others. Zau gestured toward four men from his village. The men bowed toward Zau, and Mabo and the spirits gathered, rose upright, and graciously approached Usa with a thatched stretcher. Mabo and Zau offered prayer over Usa. The six men lifted Usa, laid his body on the stretcher, and escorted him to a nearby tented area. A short time later, the six men rejoined the others.

Maik directed her energy toward the visualization and continued. Mabo would continue to be the holy leader for the area, and Zau would continue the honor for his village as Usa would have wanted. As before, these men and their partners would be the humans with spiritual answers to questions. With recorded services uploaded to the next internet. The children in the area shrilled; they could help with the recorded devices. Maik generated loving thoughts toward them. Taking turns, yes, they would all assist. Tiao felt so honored the children had behaved well and she had blown them kisses. Some children reached out to grab them and smacked them on their cheeks. Laughter was heard from children to parents, to the elders.

Akaham continued with the visualization after the roar of laughter died down. As for the children, yes indeed, what a grand era to be alive for them. Aunewu was an Ambassador, yes, but what did this entail? Aunewu was not aware of what precisely an Ambassador was, and neither had his father, whom both had looked at each other. Akaham explained through the visualization that Aunewu, like most children, should be of a free spirit. A question mark appeared on most children's foreheads and most of the parents. For the elders, they knew and winked at Akaham. For the children from the desolate territorial war areas, ripped from them was their free spirits. Aunewu was an example of that free spirit, curious, energetic, the child who never seemed to tire, well until, as his father Augustin had said—he 'fell out,' he assisted everyone, and how his kindness was contagious. The 'aha moment' registered with the children and their parents. So, the children of now were granted permission to be free, yet kindness to all was of utmost importance!

The children glanced at one another. Aunewu was precisely that; kind to all. Never did he bully anyone or ask too much from anyone; he always seemed to be right there to help. Ah, yes, exactly as they wanted to do and be; what a tremendous human example. The admiration shocked Aunewu. His father placed his hand on his shoulder and gave a light squeeze. Aunewu glanced toward his father's eyes and motioned for him to hear him. Augustin complied, and a grin crossed his face. He stood upright and hugged his son's shoulder. Maik projected the thought process on the visualization. Aunewu had asked his father if he could have permission to walk among the animals with all the children present. Augustin had not ignored him; he told him permission may not be granted. Akaham injected his thought process toward the visualization; indeed, all children needed to learn from Aunewu, Quiatua, Samuel, and others who wanted to join how kindness resonated outwards, even to the animal kingdom.

With these instructions, Maik and Akaham sent one last for all present to prepare for their journey toward their homelands. Some humans were anxious and excited and ready to return to family, friends, and the familiarity of their lives. To share all they had experienced, pass the knowledge onto others, and begin their meditation state toward the healing process. Oh, the numbers of people who needed the healing, needed the comfort, needed their newfound abilities. Some humans had felt safe and comfortable and wanted to continue living with the villagers, Mabo and Tiao, forever. With much appreciation, Mabo, Tiao, and Zau sent loving thoughts to all in the area.

Aunewu motioned for permission to communicate with Mabo, whose smile stretched across his face and granted permission. Aunewu expressed with all present no despair as these devices and the ones that will materialize will be given and shared. All gathered glanced at the device and back toward Aunewu. He went on to explain; therefore, we all stay in touch. We all keep in touch in a positive light, love, and human spirit! Whenever needed, you pick up the device, power it on as instructed, connect to this incredible thing called the 'next internet,' and look up anyone or any of us. Isn't this incredible? The elders in the area nodded toward Aunewu and his excitement, and they may not have understood the device and connection, etcetera. Still, they knew communication and visual aid was everything. The parents of the children showed concern, while Quiatua stepped forward and offered communication.

She had been unaware of this type of device before, and this thing called the 'next internet' she could not wait to dive in and keep in touch with all present. To continue communication with them, learn with them and all humans on the Earth, and share laughter and love through such a device was phenomenal to her. Quiatua explained she wanted to be the last leave, and she had not felt such loving people since her parents and siblings passed. She wanted to stay put forever and ever also!

Yet, she continued, she understood she needed to return and spread the fantastic news, healings and teach others. Also, she knew she would always return to this incredible place, these remarkable people. She loved everyone so deeply; how could she not return? She sincerely asked everyone to consider the same.

On that sentiment, Mabo bowed toward all in the area and knew through conversation with Tiao that all were welcome back. He resonated the same to all gathered, to feel free to return. He stood upright, raised his arms and head skyward, asked for Blessings from all above for those on the Earth, lowered his head, and prayed aloud. Once he ended his prayer, he gestured for all in the area that there was a feast to prepare and all should receive their nourishments together. Slowly parents helped the elders upright, and some children helped their parents upright as all cleared the area to prepare for the feast. The description of what was to be retrieved and brought to the center as energetic children jumped with the opportunity to run and retrieve. All present smiled when they heard the laughter of excitement erupt in the air.

CHAPTER 15

The following dawn arrived, and silhouettes were visible throughout the village. Some individuals were in groups, and discussions were audible among them. Most humans were designated tasks to complete before Zau and others' departure. An adorned wagon and a covering were furnished in honor of Usa for his travel with Saib and Majestic. At the same time, Zau stretched his lengthy body toward the four directions and offered praise for the glorious day of travel, the fortunes of so many grand humans present, and the presence of Onyx, who would guard them on the way to their village. Mabo and Tiao waited for his arrival at the village center as Zeus walked alongside him. They greeted and embraced one another as Tiao offered to pin the emblem upon Zau's clothing above his heart. Zau accepted graciously, bowed to Tiao, and thanked her for the intricate work, so delicate, so lovingly made that he felt the honor others had when pinned.

More humans were visible as the sun rose in the area, as group members and their companions arrived at the center with huge smiles and love in their eyes. They all felt such an honor had been bestowed upon them to have known Usa. He was indeed a gracious and loved man. Aunewu asked permission to communicate. Mabo gently touched the boy's shoulder, smiled, and granted permission. Aunewu explained he, with Augustin, had fashioned a symbol for Usa. Tears welled in all eyes in the immediate area. Mabo gestured for Aunewu to present the symbol, carefully fashioned from corn husk. The beautiful piece was intertwined with painted dots from nearby berry dye. Mabo gestured toward Zau to come closer, then placed the piece into his hands. Zau bowed toward Aunewu and Augustin, who returned the gesture. Zau offered Mabo to bless the article afterward and gestured he would place the piece on Usa for his journey. Aunewu beamed with delight as he grabbed his father's hand.

Kindness resonated with all gathered as Quiatua stepped forward to hug Zau, as the rest of the group did so. Zau felt such love he had to regain his bearings as he gripped Aunewu's shoulder for stability and let the boy know his appreciation. Villagers gathered around the center, and some offered Zau grand blessings for travel. Some provided their fashioned ornaments for Usa, as one requested permission to communicate with all. Permission granted, the older adult bowed toward all present. He gestured toward others in the area, and a soft drumbeat was audible as the others circulated the area with arms open wide. Quiet chants were heard as Mabo explained that all present should return and join the village at any given time; provisions would always be available. The drumbeat and soft chant completed, the others bowed to all present, stood upright, and blew kisses toward all. The golden light of the Great Source showered downward onto the village.

Some humans left the village center with peace in their spirits that illuminated brighter as they walked toward the outskirts. The tremendous final journey for Usa was underway while a respectful silence resonated throughout the area. Saib signaled to Majestic to move forward. Once united with Zau, he climbed upon the wagon and toward where Usa lay, uncovered the upper half of linen cloth, pinned the symbol onto Usa's clothing above his heart, bowed his head, and prayed silently. Zau placed other fashioned items on Usa's linen cloth as Zau covered Usa's upper half with the fabric and placed more items. Such a loving and human tribute from so many in the area, tears stood in Zau's eyes as he climbed from the wagon. Then, with a respectful bow toward Mabo, he stood upright and motioned for Saib to begin the journey toward his village with the others.

Aunewu was impressed by the honor of silence for the great man and wonderful human who reminded him of Simounte; then, he realized they were kindred spirits. He looked around at the group members and their companions; he eyed the insignia on each chest, looked toward and felt his on his chest. Quiatua was the first to realize the boy's longing to travel homeward. With a massive smile, she approached Aunewu, lightly grabbed his shoulders in her hands, and gave a light squeeze as she communicated now was time for the animals. Aunewu felt the warmth of love. He grinned wildly at Quiatua and expressed to all; can this be when we visit with the animals, he wondered? Without further delay, Mabo signaled a villager to sound the horned instrument.

Within moments villagers approached the center. Mabo communicated to the guest, group, and villagers undertaking other tasks to prepare for travel; the children of all and those who wanted were welcome to walk with Aunewu and Zeus. Elders smiled and began a line toward the outskirts. Children glanced toward their parents and elders; when given all is well, you may join gesture, the children raced toward them. Most humans in the village joined Aunewu and Zeus, and those who stayed continued their task of preparations. Samuel did not hesitate to grab a recording device and joined the boy and Zeus. He could not shake thoughts of the story he had read of a youth in the jungle befriended by a feline and other animals as a smile crept across his face.

Katerina, Suri, and Quiatua were side-by-side with Aunewu and Zeus, while Warec, Augustin, Eusia, Rundda, Mabo, and Tiao filed into the procession. Aunewu began communication with Zeus as they walked into the forest area. So many surprises came to some present when they heard Zeus' thought process—an intelligent and beautiful species, sleek and perceptive of their surroundings. Zeus was curious why humans on Earth took so long to approach the animal kingdom in kindness. Not all humans, Zeus corrected himself, but most. Quiatua expressed to Zeus and all others that it was a shame most humans did not appreciate the harmony. A chuckled purr was audible from Zeus as Aunewu reached toward his scruff and gave an affectionate tussle. Slowly animals from different species were visible, and Zeus signaled for the humans to kneel. No harm shall come, he explained, be in the silence; the animals will choose whom they will go toward. Most humans present were astounded by an 'aha moment' and fell into quiet and passive surrender, and next, the animals came, as Samuel recorded.

Chapter 16

Omarya saw the progress of all involved in the village, and the time had arrived for the 'guest' to begin their journey homeward. He rallied support from numerous Spirit Guides and Ascended Healers. The Ascended Masters placed communications with those families and associates in regions where the guests were to travel homeward. Preparations were underway to receive them, grant calm and restful peace upon arrival, and celebrations could begin afterward. All bowed in respect toward the Masters. Most who communicated with the Masters were elated to have those humans returning to them and would wait for further instructions, if any.

Maik had communicated with Omarya that those strong enough to travel would leave later in the day on Earth. The ones who needed further healing would stay under the attention of Mabo, Tiao, Eusia, and Rundda for a short time. Omarya agreed all humans were necessary once they arrived in their regions. Yes, some acclimation would be required, yet he wanted what the Great Source intended for those to speak their truth. For the humans to have been rescued and freed of oppression, they also had been taken to a safe place where: love, health, and peace were of utmost importance to them all. The Great Source they were familiar with, prayed to, and admired highly answered their needs. These same humans would not hesitate to tell others to trust the release, the freedom, and most of all, trust the process. They would experience the genuine care of their Great Source, the all-knowing, all-loving, and all aware.

The Great Source had appointed the other Ambassadors to prepare for their departure. All provisions were available, and the Guides would accompany them during their travels. The Ambassadors were needed in their regions and could communicate amongst themselves via the next internet that was in full use. Once other humans gained their knowledge, skills, and experiences, the Ambassadors would reconvene in various regions around the World during a yearly summit. These explanations would come from their Ascended Masters. The ongoing communication for the Ambassadors would be, as granted from the Great Source, with Akaham and Maik. The humans would feel no restlessness as they returned to their homes, all was well, and Great Source was pleased.

The Ambassadors' learning was immense. Katerina and Suri would decide upon New Zealand or Katerina's homeland, Ukraine. However, before deciding, they would communicate with fellow scientists and mathematicians on the Antarctica continent. The role of scientists and mathematicians in Antarctica had been a revolving opportunity; therefore, new humans would visit and work, eventually leaving the area. Their communication on the following internet supplied these women's talents to go forward forever on the continent. The women would be allowed to discover other continents as Ambassadors. Eventually, the other Ambassadors would have the same opportunity.

Bittersweet for Quiatua, yet she was to return to her region in North America. Her learning, skills, and knowledge were of utmost importance for the humans and her maturity. She now had opportunities to share, care for and support other humans. She could look forward to a lifetime of others seeking her. In addition, other humans would record her efforts and teaching. Like the other Ambassadors, she needed the appreciation of human interaction. Her Ascended Master was well pleased with her progress and had guaranteed her Spirit Guide, Azna, that she would mature in leaps and bounds. The recent experience had provided her with personal growth, and she did not fear human connections with others as when she was alone in the tree-dwelling.

Samuel was to return to Australia and communicate his experiences firsthand to those in the zoo. He would prove his growth in the animal kingdom and mirror the knowledge he learned from Quiatua and Aunewu. He would also experience sheer acceleration when other humans had the 'aha moment' with the animals. These interactions and his continued studies of the animal kingdom and herbology would be recorded and uploaded to the next internet. With great pride, his Ascended Master, Luna, anticipated the teaching moments ahead for Samuel. She was well pleased with the progress and confidence Samuel had acquired with his presence here in this peaceful place. She looked forward to the sense of peace surrounding Samuel as it oozed toward other humans he encountered and when back at the zoo. Australia may not have been his homeland, but now Samuel felt a kinship to the land, people, and animals.

Back in their homeland, Aunewu and Augustin were significantly missed. Their long journey home was communicated through Dyne, Aunewu's Ascended Master. Haou, Aunewu's mother, knew he and her spouse were in great company. So much of her realization had shifted over time while they were gone. She had come to know her own Ascended Master Lio and her Guides. Haou prayed and meditated daily, thankful for the Great Source and their trust in her and her family. Aunewu would arrive with such energy and tales of his adventures and probably had grown a foot taller. His maturity would have gained such experiences she could not fathom. To wrap her arms around both would be peace on Earth to her. She knew a period of adjustment awaited Aunewu and Augustin, as not all humans were considered Ambassadors. Aunewu's kindness to all humans, animals, plants, and tree life would resonate beyond their village, region, and this continent; she blushed with pride and exhilaration for both.

Warec had communicated to his Ascended Master, Yellow, that, indeed, at first, he was reluctant to acknowledge the vision and words. Unwilling to even accept Yellow and the other Masters that had brought the vision and words. At his age and sophistication, he could not understand why he even called and booked the flight to some unknown airport in South America. But boy, was he glad he did! He had explained that he had come to believe no other time in this lifetime or his other lifetimes that he needed humankind. His experiences, skills, and knowledge were grand prior, but now he understood what he had acquired quickly. Warec had meditated like never before. He saw visions of so many humans aided by his written word and recorded seminars on herbology. How most manufactured medication could receive help from herbs. He communicated to the other Ambassadors, Masters, Healers, and Guides; he was renewed from his experience and could not wait to get cracking on the following internet with all the knowledge.

Mabo and his beloved Tiao would look forward to the Ambassadors' arrival to their homelands safe and sound. They had much anticipation of where Katerina and Suri would settle; they had the opportunity to know the two women in the hours they spent with them during conversations of religion, the spirit world, grace, meditation, prayer, healings, and pure bliss that astounded them. They were ecstatic to partake in the journey with all these incredible humans. They both knew each one would journey back to the village, where the destination was always about love and respect. Respect as each one found their bearings, for them to lean on one another, learn, experience, and share the teachings. Mabo and Tiao never fathomed they would travel to different destinations around the World for summits. What an experience for them to have together; they could not wait until their first summit!

Eusia and Rundda were delighted to share some unforeseen news. Peluan, her Ascended Master, drew her an image in a cloud. The image depicted Eusia back in her homeland, pregnant, not only one baby but two! Rundda was teary- eyed when he approached Mabo and asked the instrument sounded. Without further delay, the instrument sounded. Rundda bowed to all gathered, stood upright, grasped his beloved Eusia by the waist, turned her sideways gently, and showed a plump belly with a pillow under a cloth. Some humans perceived his intentions immediately, while others took time to digest the demonstration. Cheers erupted throughout the village while Eusia blushed and patted Rundda's hand and the pillow. What a wonderful couple to have such a blessing bestowed upon them! Rundda demonstrated two fingers as his other hand pointed toward the pillow belly. More cheers erupted as some humans wiped tears from their eyes. Indeed, the Ambassadors' future looked bright as golden rays of light filled the area sent by the Great Source.

Epilouge

Insight

The Bridge was introduced by a vision and words for seven individuals, one from each continent, blessed beyond their comprehension. For them and their companions, the journey forward was phenomenal. No denial that there was one source: Great Source, the Omnipotent. There were many names, paths, many belief systems to the One; there was only One. Whatever the human named their belief systems for Omnipotent, whatever the pathway that led toward this belief system, there was no wrong name, version, or path. For this Great Source, there was a duality of masculine and feminine energy. The same power initially granted human, animal, plant, water, and tree life on Earth.

For each human who received the vision and words, they embarked on a catechetical journey with a destination area that honored: love, trust, healing, care, and respect. Their companions were blessed and welcomed to go with the humans. The Great Source did not admire the conditions on the Earth, and as read from the words, they devised a way of abolishing evil, sinister, and destructive intentions. They could have destroyed the Earth; however, their choices were to reset the humans experience. The Great Source believed in human life forms on this Earth; they wanted humans to amend their actions, thoughts, beliefs, or non-belief.

For the humans who believed in a higher energy source, whichever way they considered their One, who had lived by principles, integrity, and care of all inhabitants and the animal kingdom on the Earth, the blessings continued for them. They received three-fold the knowledge, learnings, and skills from Ascended Masters, Healers, Guides, the Blessed Ones, and the incredible Power Animals. The transition of the Earth came to be through the prayers, meditation, actions, and thought processes of these humans. The blessing for these humans was other humans who were perhaps non-believers or on the 'proverbial fence' began to realize, understand, and act. These humans saw a significant change unlike any other they had experienced.

From Omarya overseeing the counsel of Ascended Masters to Akaham and Maik to the Spirit Guides and Ascended Healers—all was well. They had exhaustive effort of energy expelled when they contributed to the transition. Not without the constant ability to communicate with the Blessed Ones and Great Source. Through the One, all was possible, and the overseers became charged with the outcome of the efforts. While extinguishing any negative human energy, thought processes and actions were dissolved. What a great life to be alive during this part of the process. As the atmosphere cleared from pollution, the seas became clean and rolled unobstructed by floating debris pollutants. When humans appreciated the interaction with the animal kingdom, plant, and tree life, as their existence expanded, their mindset switched from 'just make it through one more day.'

Humans grasped the positive energy that oozed from the following internet rather than darkness, evil and sinister destruction for all eyes to see. The evil-doers wanted the humans to take the negativity into their essence more than anything, yet the higher energy source squashed it like an unwanted parasite. The earlier internet grew its lifeblood from the negativity, while the Great Source had no issue when they dismantle it. They knew so many professions, healers, teachers, and students relied upon its purpose of goodness in the World. Their confidence in humankind to gain access, record, and upload to the following internet so the transition could be front and center would deem the internet to be positive energy only.

Great Source recognized human health and ailment without a doubt. However, the intention was for humans to help humans in natural and profound ways. Using crystal, herbal, traditional customs and acknowledgment, prayer, and meditation was crucial to their intervention with humans. Great Source saw how wise and advanced humanity had become, but relying entirely upon substitute medications and treatments missed the point. Humans needed human contact, practices of Reiki, massage and sound therapy, incense and sage burning, and oil and milk bathing were some of the lost arts of medication, and they wanted humans to rediscover the natural wonders of the World in medicine.

The title of Ambassador held high honor, not to be mistaken with a position of a human having—all significant knowledge. Great Source appointed all Ambassadors and their companions to continue their growth through shared understanding with others, education, experiences, and most of all, word-of-mouth through the following internet. The Ambassadors and all humans were in reach of immense support through the Ascended Masters, Healers, Guides, and the beloved Power Animals. The title was not only the Ambassador could pray or meditate toward the Blessed Ones, Akaham, Maik, or Great Source, but all humans would. The Ambassadors were chosen for controlled order. When a message was to be received by a human, the Ambassador was the human. When an urgent message required a response or a request made, the Ambassador was the human.

Reasoning the urgency to scrub the internet and issue the next version in a positive light was of utmost importance so humankind knew there were safeguards in place. Human societies around the World adapted to inclusion with all individuals, their belief systems, their cultures, and their self-identification. No longer was there need for division, ridicule, hate, war, or death due to religion, belief system, or thought process. All individuals were encouraged toward the higher and greater good for themselves and humanity. Human feelings of self- ridicule and low self-esteem were no longer considered an issue for many people. Every human offered a place in the World. They resonated with the light of the Great Source; individuals became like-minded within the World. The World gained significant strives due to the efforts of all.

About the Author

L T Bailey has been an intuitive writer since she was a child. While encountering a variety of readings during adulthood, she ultimately founded and became the coordinator for a group studying the global belief system. Three years into the experience, L T was called to join the church, Unity of Pensacola, Florida. Bridging Between is her first book.

Printed in the United States
by Baker & Taylor Publisher Services